The Secret World of Polly Flint

Helen Cresswell

Five Leaves Publications
www.fiveleaves.co.uk

The Secret World of Polly Flint
by Helen Cresswell

Published in 2008
by Five Leaves Publications,
PO Box 8786, Nottingham NG1 9AW
info@fiveleaves.co.uk
www.fiveleaves.co.uk

The Secret World of Polly Flint
was first published in 1982 by Faber and Faber

ISBN: 978 1 905512 48 5

Five Leaves acknowledges financial support
from Arts Council England

Five Leaves is a member of Inpress
(www.inpressbooks.co.uk),
representing independent publishers

Typeset by Four Sheets Design and Print
Printed in Great Britain

The Secret World of Polly Flint

Chapter 1

Once upon a time — and I mean last week, or last year — there was a girl called Polly Flint, and one day she saw an angel. It was the strangest thing. She had gone into the field to pick flowers, and was quite alone. Then she tired of this, and instead, started to spin. Round and round she whirled with her arms outspread. Soon she was dizzy and fell sideways into the long grass. And she lay there, face upturned to the sky and a queer roaring in her head, and that was when she saw the angel.

He was tall as a giant and tongued with flame and he went swiftly, so that his hair streamed. He went along close by like a rushing wind. Polly came up on her elbows to watch him go with wings bristling and bare feet that touched the grasses but did not stir them.

"Oh my!" said Polly Flint softly to herself. "Oh, my good gracious!"

The whole world was a brilliant, singing green and amongst all that green went that bright angel. The shine of him was too much for her to bear so she closed her eyes, and when she opened them again, he had gone. Back she lay again with her eyes closed and wondered what it all meant. She had never in her life dreamed that she might see an angel in the fields, but now she had, and she wondered why.

She went straight home and told them.

"I saw an angel in the field — just this minute ago!"

"What's that?" said Alice, who was making bread with plenty of noise and thumping.

5

"An angel, Mam! I saw one in the field, tall and flaming — and ooh, beautiful he was!"

"Now come along, Polly," said Alice. "You know you never did."

"I did! I saw an angel!"

"Now don't you go saying things like that!"

"Why, why mustn't I say it?"

"Because you just don't *see* angels, Polly."

"Why?"

"Because there's no such — because you don't!"

"I did, I did! I was just lying there, after I'd been twizzling, and he came striding right past me — I could see the ruffling of his hem and his bare feet and —".

"Twizzling?" said Alice. "*Twizzling*? You can't see a deal straight when you've been twizzling, that I *do* know."

"Could've been the sun shafting through the grasses, Polly," said Tom "Rum tricks, the sun can play."

"Well, I know it wasn't," said Polly, kicking her feet against the table.

"And the less twizzling you do, the better," Alice told her. "Dizzy enough, without that. Polly, *don't*!"

Polly stopped kicking her feet.

"I'm going right back," she told them. "See if he's still there."

"And that's very likely!" called Alice after her. The door banged "Polly — *don't*!"

"You're always Polly don't-ing her," Tom said "Let her *have* her angel."

"Oh, *you*, Tom Flint!" Alice was kneading the dough now, slapping and pulling with a will. "Bad as she is, you are. Where she gets it from, I daresay. Not from my side, that is a fact. You'll be saying next that

6

you believe in her blessed angel."

"I do believe that she believes she saw it," Tom said carefully.

"There you are then!" said Alice. "Mazed as cuckoos, the pair of you!"

"I'll go on after her," Tom said. "Do with stretching my legs."

He went out and saw that one of his pigeons was just flying back to her roost, and stopped to give her water.

"There, my pretty." He stroked her soft neck. "There's a clever lass!"

Down in the field Polly was looking in vain for her angel.

"I'll try twizzling again," she thought.

Round and round she spun, fast as before, and down she fell. But all she saw was a blur of green and gold, and twice more she twirled and then felt sick. This time when she opened her eyes, she did see a tall figure, and squealed.

"Dad! You gave me a real fright!"

"Thought you'd've seen me coming," he said. "But too busy twizzling. Never took *me* for an angel, did you?"

Polly sat up, her head still reeling.

"Oh Dad!" she said. "Don't *you* start!"

"Here, let's give you a hand up," and he pulled her to her feet.

"Do you believe that anything can happen in the world?" she asked. "Because I do, after today. Anything at all."

"Aye, I believe that, I suppose," he said.

"I bet you'd have made one of your rhymes about it."

"I believe I should," he agreed.

7

"Well then," said Polly, "that's what *I* shall do. That way, I'll keep him for ever."

"That's the way," Tom said. "Good."

"So shall you help me with some rhymes, to start me off?"

"Come on, then," he said. "Let's see... flame, came... yes, and scene, green...."

"Pass... grass," supplied Polly.

And so the pair of them walked on back home, happily exchanging rhymes, as they often did. Tom was a coal miner but he was also a poet. He said that the two jobs fitted together very well. When he read out his finished poems Alice would sometimes sniff, and say it was the first time she'd heard of a rhyming miner, but secretly she was proud of him, and so was Polly. His other great loves were his pigeons and his fishing.

He kept the pigeons, eight of them, in a special wooden house he had made in the back yard. He knew them all by name, and they would fly to his call. He was out there with them when Polly came to show him her finished rhyme. She'd been sitting upstairs on her bed sucking her pencil for nearly an hour.

"Dad! I've done it!"

"Good lass. Hear it, can I?"

She drew a deep breath.

"It's not very good," she told him. "Nothing, really. And nobody could *ever* tell how tall and bright and startling that angel was to me. But anyway...

"As I lay in the green green grass
I saw a tall white angel pass.
Rushing like the wind he came
With feet of snow and hair of flame."

"Good!" cried Tom. "Good!"

"There's one more line," she told him:

"And the world will never be the same."

There was a pause, filled only by the soft purr of contented pigeons.

"Well, I reckon that's something, our Poll," Tom said at last. "I reckon that's really something."

"Are they all in?" Polly asked, meaning the pigeons.

He nodded.

"You love them old birds, don't you, Dad?"

He nodded again.

"It's something pr'aps you wouldn't understand. But I reckon there's a reason why we go in for birds, round these parts. When you're down there under the ground, hours without a glimpse of daylight, and working sometimes in tunnels that narrow you can hardly stretch — well, the thought of them birds, winging and flying and making patterns in that great huge sky somewhere up there — well, that's a good thought. One you can hold on to down there."

"I think I *can* see," said Polly. "Even if I've never been down there. What's it *like* in a coal mine, Dad?"

"Shut off from the world," he said, "and with a warm wind blowing."

"A wind?" Polly was amazed. "A *warm* wind?"

"Hot, and dry, and dusty," he said. "You'd know you was down there, even if you was blindfold."

His face was hidden. He was all the while mending the netting on a door frame. Polly watched him, and thought,

"I'm glad he's my Dad. He's as brave as a lion because he goes down into the depths of the earth.

And he makes rhymes, *and* he believes in angels."

Then Alice came to the back door.

"Just look at the pair of you!" she said. "Mooning over them dratted birds! Are you wanting any tea, or aren't you?"

Tom turned and gave his slow, wide grin.

"We're wanting," he said.

In the days that followed Polly Flint did not see another angel, and nor did she ever again, for that matter. But when she had written that last line of her rhyme, "And the world will never be the same," she was right. She now knew, for absolutely certain, that the world was more mysterious than she had ever supposed it. She felt all the time as if she were on the very fringes of another world, a wider one, and would catch glimpses of it — only fleeting, perhaps only for a few seconds, but glimpses all the same. She began to spend even more of her time in the fields and woods beyond the little town. She would sit and string daisies by the hour and time would pass in a dream. And then sometimes, when she lifted her eyes, the world would seem to blur, as if it were only a reflection, and strangest of all, one day the town beyond seemed to melt away and leave an empty landscape, fields, trees, sky. But even as she stared, the town began to come again, and she rubbed her eyes hard.

"Haven't been twizzling *this* time," she thought. "Threading daisies ain't like twizzling. Can make you dizzy, though, in a way. Sick of it, anyhow!"

Then she got up and ran to the little wood beyond, where sometimes she would think she heard distant voices echoing, threading the clear whistling of the birds. And the echoes seemed to be calling her name — "Polly! Polly!" Not a word did she say of this to

Alice and Tom.

And then something happened that was to change their whole lives. It was a day in April, a day of daffodil yellow sun and the first calls of cuckoos, and never a day you would expect to end in a terrible darkness.

Polly came running down to the kitchen where Alice was giving Tom breakfast. He was a big man, and he ate heartily.

"Mam, Dad — just heard the first cuckoo!"

"You spend much more time mooning in them fields, and *you'll* end up cuckoo," Alice told her. "Nip and fetch the milk in, there's a good girl."

"Fishing weather," Tom said, as she came back in. "Perfect."

"Oh Dad! Can I come, can I?"

"Can you what?" Alice whipped round from the sink. "Can you *what*, Polly Flint? School, my girl, is where you're going. I never heard of such a thing!"

"A *morning* don't make much difference," Polly said. "Don't learn much in just a morning."

"Hmph!" Alice tossed her head. "And that depends who you are. Learn plenty in a morning, if you put your mind to it."

Polly poured a golden shower of cornflakes and kicked her feet against the table.

"I daresay the odd morning here or there don't make that much difference, Alice," said Tom.

"That child ain't going fishing, she's going to school, and there's an end to it!" said Alice. "Polly — *don't*!"

Polly poured milk on her cornflakes, and thought, "Might as well be *called* Polly Don't, number of times it gets said. Not Polly Flint at all — Polly Don't."

"You on nights, Dad?" she asked out loud.

"Afternoons," he told her.

"Might as well say goodnight to you now, then," she said. "You'll be gone when I get back from school."

"Why, then, goodnight, Polly," he said gravely.

"Goodnight, Dad," replied Polly, and they both began to laugh, while Alice cried, "Well, if now I haven't heard it all — goodnight at breakfast!"

But in the end she laughed, too, which was good, because it was to be a long time before they were all to laugh together again.

That night when Alice came up to say goodnight to Polly, she said, "I do believe I forgot to say goodnight to you at breakfast, so I thought I'd best come up and say it now, if it's not too late!" and they both laughed again.

"I don't like it when Dad's on nights," said Polly. "I never get read to."

"I have offered," said Alice, "and I can't do more."

"I'm sorry to say, Mam, it's not the same," Polly told her. She giggled.

"Little madam!" Alice told her, and stooped to kiss her.

"Don't like to think of Dad down there in the dark, either," Polly said.

"Little goose! Makes no difference day or night, down there — nor winter or summer either, come to that!"

"*Seems* different," said Polly obstinately. "To me it does."

"Off with that light now." Alice leaned over to it and spotted tell tale crumbs on the table. "Here — I see you've had biscuits up here again. I've told you before, Polly — don't!"

"Sorry," said Polly. "I'll try to remember. Night

then, Mam."

"Night, Polly. Sleep tight."

She went out and Polly turned over on her side.

"Polly don't from morning till night," she thought. "First thing in the morning and last thing at night. Polly don't!"

She closed her eyes and thought of Tom working away down there under the ground.

"Might be under this very house at this very minute," she thought. "How did he say it was down there...? Shut off from the world, with a warm wind blowing... queer... *cold* I should've thought it would've been..."

Her thoughts faded into a haze of silently unfolding pictures and then they, too, faded. And in her sleep she may or may not have heard the unaccustomed wail of the pit siren, but afterwards she thought she had.

She woke with a start to the sound of voices in the kitchen below. Something about those voices frightened her. They were urgent and raised in a way she had never heard before. Still dazed, she thought, "But it's dark — it's still night time! What's happening?"

She stretched out to turn on the bedside lamp and looked at the clock. Nearly eleven o'clock. Downstairs, someone was crying.

Swaying a little, half asleep, Polly went down the stairs and into the kitchen. It seemed to be full of people. Then there was absolute silence. She stood in the doorway and looked at the faces of George and Betty Garret from over the road, and Ted and Doris King from next door, Bill Stevens, and a man whose face she knew but could not put a name to.

Everyone was looking at her with such strange

expressions — looks of fear, sorrow and pity — that for a moment they all seemed strangers, even her own mother.

"Oh Polly!" It was Alice, white-faced and scared-looking. "Come along, my pet!"

She moved swiftly forwards and put her arms round Polly, holding her tight. Then she stroked her hair, very hard and fast.

"What, Mam?" Polly was bewildered. "What's the matter?"

"Polly, you've got to be very brave. You see —"

Polly screamed, "Dad, dad!" She *must* have heard that wailing siren, or must have dreamed it.

"Hush now, hush my darling. We don't know yet."

"What's happened? Is he down there still? Oh Dad!"

She wailed, and held on tight to Alice, smelling the starch of her apron. (Alice rarely took off her apron, until she went to bed.) People were talking again now, all at once.

"Now you must be brave, Polly, you hear me? I'm going now, with George and Betty, to the pit head. I'll be there, then, when they bring him up."

"I'm coming, Mam, I am."

"No, Polly. It's late at night — and no place for you, anyhow."

"But Mam —"

"I want you to be a good girl, as your Dad would want you to be. I want you to go back to bed, and try to go to sleep. Doris'll stay down here till I get back."

"I can't sleep! I shall never sleep!"

"Come along, love. I'll take you up now."

She took Polly's hand and they went together up the stairs and back to her tumbled bed.

"I'll ask Doris to fetch you up some warm milk,"

14

Alice promised before she went.

Polly very meekly climbed into bed, and allowed herself to be tucked back in. But the moment Alice had reached the foot of the stairs, Polly was out again. Nimbly and silently she dressed, hardly noticing the tears that were running down her cheeks and splashing down.

Down the stairs she tiptoed, glad of the hubbub in the kitchen. The front door was directly opposite her. Carefully she clicked back the latch, gently eased open the door. Then she was outside, in the shock of the cold air, and pulled the door gently to behind her.

Then began the long run through the night, through the narrow, terraced streets to the pit head. The pavements were empty, the windows of the houses blank, but that meant nothing to Polly Flint. She saw only a picture of her father's face, black with coal dust (though she had never seen it so) and heard only her own gasping breath and the sound of her feet thudding on the cobbles.

She paused at the top of Parson Hill for breath, and a car came by, and she caught a glimpse of her mother's pale face. Her eyes were fixed and sightless, and Polly guessed that Alice, too, was seeing Tom's face instead of the world.

Now it was downhill all the way to the pit, she could see the floodlights below and the flashing blue lights in the pit yard. And now her thoughts ran fast to the pattern of her feet, "Let him be all right, let him be all right, let him not be dead, let him not be dead..."

She saw Alice at once in the pit yard, standing in a huddle of others under a pool of light. Straight to her Polly ran and for a second time was caught and held tightly.

"Mam, mam, I had to come!"

"Hush, my darling, it's all right. Of course you did."

"Is he safe? Have you heard?"

"There are three of them hurt. They're bringing them up now."

Polly would remember that wait all her life long. She'd remember the wide yard and the sharp, criss-crossing shadows under the flood lights and beyond the darkness, moon and stars invisible. She'd remember, too, her father being brought at last on a stretcher. Alice and she leant over him. Polly had never before seen her father with the dust of the pit on him. His face was blackened, and the hands that lay limply on the blankets.

"Tom!" Alice put out one of her own hands to clasp his. "Tom, love — it's me, Alice!"

"He'll not hear you, love," said one of the men.

"The doctor's been and injected him, see."

"Oh! Oh!" Tears of disappointment squeezed from her eyes. "How bad is he?"

It was then that Doris and Ted arrived, in a terrible taking.

"There she is!" they cried, seeing Polly. And then there was confusion as Alice asked leave to go with Tom to the hospital, and Polly was sent sobbing home again.

It was a sad night's work, though not so bad as it might have been. Tom would live, though he was the worst hurt of the three. At the moment he could not move his legs at all. This might come right, they said, in time.

"It will!" said Polly fiercely, when she was told. "It will, it will!"

She would not believe that Tom, who was tall and

strong and went with a long, lank stride, might never have the use of his legs again.

She went to see him as he lay there and his long slow grin had altered not a bit, and she tried not to think of his legs lying useless under that iron cage. He made her promise to look after Alice.

"For you know how she is," he said. "Try to stop her from getting low, shall you?"

Polly agreed, and did her best in the days that followed. She ran errands, laid a table without being asked, and helped look after Tom's pigeons, with Ted next door. The familiar sight of them tumbling out of the sky, and the sheer comfortableness of them as they blinked and purred in their warm straw, somehow made the world as it should be again for Polly, and she spent hours talking to them.

"My Dad's going to get well, you know," she would tell them. "He'll be back to throw you your corn, never you fear. You won't catch my Dad spending his life flat on his back. Mam says so, too. Says it's not in his nature. 'T'ain't, either!"

The pigeons would gaze roundly at her, and seem to nod their heads. At any rate, Polly knew they understood. It was one day when she was out talking to them that she met the coal miner. It was the strangest thing. One minute he was not there and then, when she looked, he was. She smiled at him and he smiled back, and his teeth and eyes flashed white out of his sooty face.

"Fond of these old birds, ain't you, lass?" he said, and Polly nodded.

"And so'm I." He reached and very gently lifted one and held it cradled between his two hands.

"Good, when you're down there underground, to

think of 'em up here. Go through that huge sky as if they'd their own map, inside their heads."

"That's just what my Dad says," Polly told him.

"Then your Dad's right," the coal miner told her. "And I reckon it must do him good, and all, to think on 'em now. I reckon he dreams on these birds as a prisoner dreams on freedom."

"Oooh, I'd give anything to be able to fly," Polly said. "Think — swooping and soaring, all the quietness up there, and the space!"

"Well, then, and so we all *can* fly," said the coal miner.

"What do you mean?" Polly asked.

"Inside of our heads," he told her. "Fly wherever we've a mind to. Could tell your Dad that. He'll know what you mean, like enough."

"Oh, he will," Polly assured him. "There's a lot goes on inside my Dad's head. He can make rhymes, you know."

"Well, can he now?" said the miner. "That's good, then. That's very good."

At that moment Alice's voice came from the scullery.

"Polly? You out there?" Polly turned.

"Here, Mam!"

"Come along, will you? You're not near ready, and we shall miss the bus."

"Coming!" Polly turned back to explain to the coal miner that she and Alice were going to visit Tom, but he had gone.

"Well!" said Polly Flint. "*That's* rum!" and she walked slowly back into the house, shaking her head.

"You do spend a deal of time with them birds," said Alice. "Get your hair brushed, will you, and your other shoes on."

18

"I was just talking to a coal miner," Polly said.

"Oh yes? Who was that, then?"

"Well, that's the funny thing. I don't know. I felt as if I knew him, but I didn't. Not to know his name, anyhow."

Alice was not really listening. She was checking her basket, in case she had forgotten something.

"Soap... clean pyjamas... library books... mints... butterscotch..."

So Polly saved the rest of her story until she could tell the pair of them. Tom's first question was nearly always after his birds.

"Oh, they're smashing," Polly told him.

"She spends more time talking to them birds than she does to me," said Alice. "There's some'd take offence."

But she smiled as she said it, to indicate that she herself did not fall into any such category.

"And listen, Dad, I met a coal miner today!"

"Well, I'll go to the foot of our stairs," said Tom. "A coal miner! Imagine!"

"No, Dad, listen. I call him that because I didn't know his name."

"Then how d'you know he *was* a miner?" Alice demanded. "Got a badge on his front, had he, with 'coal miner' wrote on it?"

"Well, that was the queer thing," Polly admitted. "The more I've thought of it, the queerer it seems. You see..."

She looked backwards and forwards from Alice's face to Tom's, and then back again. Should she tell them? She had told about the angel, and look what had happened. But you couldn't bracket a coal miner with an *angel*...

"Come on, then, love," said Tom.

19

"We — ell... he had a helmet on, see. Yes, and sort of overalls — oh, and funny pad things on his knees."

"In his pit gear," said Tom, looking at Alice.

"I suppose... and — and his face was all black and grimy, but it gave him the nicest look, because his eyes were so white, and his teeth!"

"Oh, *I* see," said Alice. "We're in the same category as that blessed angel, a while back!"

"Oh, I *knew* you'd say that!" Polly was close to tears.

"Hold on," said Tom. "What else were you going to tell us about your miner?"

"What he said. What he said about the birds."

"And what was that?"

"Well — first he said nearly exactly what you said, Dad. You know about being good to think about the birds swooping and flying when you're cooped up down there in the mine."

"Aye. I remember."

"And then he said that *you* could fly, as well, Dad."

"Very likely!" sniffed Alice. "Walk'd satisfy me, let alone fly!"

"He meant inside your head, Dad. And he said it'd do you good while you're lying here, and that you could fly wherever you've a mind to."

"Then he was right, Polly. I can. And I do."

"There's not a word either of you says makes sense to me," said Alice. "I sometimes wonder if I belong in this family."

"You belong," Tom told her. "The likes of Polly and me, we need the likes of you, to keep us right ends up."

"Haven't made a deal of a job keeping *you* right ends up," Alice said.

"Now, Alice love, that's daft. That's plain daft, and you know it is."

Alice heaved a deep sigh.

"Am I to tell her what we've decided, then?" she asked.

"We'll tell her now," Tom said.

Polly saw a kind of shadow pass over his pale face, and cried, "What? What is it?"

"It's a big thing," said Tom slowly. "But not too big."

"We're to move, Polly," said Alice.

"Move? Move house?" She saw by their faces she was right, and in the moment felt her world shiver and rock and splinter.

They were to leave home and go and stop with Aunt Em at Wellow.

"But you don't *like* Aunt Em!" cried Polly.

"Rubbish!" said Alice flatly. "She's family, and it's family you need at times like this."

They went on to explain matters to her, and Polly could see that they had hatched a good deal without letting her in on things. It seemed that Tom would never again be able to work down the pit, however things worked out. The doctors had said that he could come out of hospital if he could be looked after at home.

"And that'll mean a deal of lifting," Alice said. "And that's where Em comes in."

Polly could see that to go to Wellow and have Tom at home was better than to stop, and have him in hospital. But what she really wanted was neither of those things. What she wanted was to stop, and for Tom not only to be home, but walking, as well.

"I've forgotten what your face looks like, the right way up," she told him.

"What's it like, at Wellow?" she asked Alice that night.

21

"Right enough," she said. "There's a big park, with a lake. Oh — and a maypole. A maypole twice as high as a house, and striped like a barber's pole. And a golden weathercock on top."

"Oh!" Polly gave a little gasp. "I think I've seen it! Have I?"

"Did go there with us, once," Alice told her. "But you were ever so little. I should hardly think you'd have remembered."

"I can see it," Polly said, "in my mind's eye. If I *don't* remember, then I must have dreamt it. Will they dance round it? It's nearly May Day now!"

"Oh, they'll do that, I should think," said Alice. "Fancy to be Queen of the May, do you?"

Polly was intent on her own thoughts, frowning a little. Then her face lightened.

>*"A maypole in the month of May*
>*Is magical — or so they say!"*

Alice shook her head.

"Just made that up, have you?"

Polly nodded.

"Just a phase you're going through, it's to be hoped," said Alice. "One in the family already, thank you. Can be doing without two."

"I like doing it," said Polly, on her dignity now. "I might do it forever, for as long as I live. And I might get better and better at it, till I'm the top poet in England. Except Dad, of course. Is Aunt Em much older than you?"

"Ten years," Alice told her. "Bossed me terrible, when I was little."

She started to talk about the old days, just as Polly had meant her to. She was still at it when Polly went to bed.

"Not to mention the time she boxed my ears, because I'd lost my glove..."

"And then you *found* it again," supplied Polly with delight. "Found it by the laurels, by the front gate..."

"...and then Mam boxed *her* ears," finished Alice, not without satisfaction even now, after nearly forty years.

"Will she try to boss you now, d'you think?" asked Polly, as she drew the bedclothes up to her chin.

"She certainly won't be boxing my ears," said Alice.

"You've never boxed mine, have you, Mam?"

"People don't, not these days," said Alice. "Had your bottom smacked plenty of times."

Polly giggled.

"Light straight out, now," said Alice. "And tomorrow you'll have to set about sorting this room out. We could have a jumble sale of our own, the stuff you've got."

"What — you mean throw things *out*?" Polly was aghast.

"There's stuff in this room you've had since you were a baby," Alice said.

When she had gone, Polly gazed about the room by the light that shafted in from the landing.

"It's you she means," she said to the row of faces watching from the top of her wardrobe and bookshelves. "You, old fox, and you, giraffe, and you, old one-eyed Lucy!"

She felt coming the tears she had been fighting back ever since they had told her.

"Don't want to go to Wellow!" she thought. "Or hateful old Aunt Em!"

And so she sobbed a little for the old faces and the

23

old places, for everything she would leave behind and perhaps never see again. The back yard, with its criss-crossing pigeons and their lovely, day-long purr, the willow at the river where Tom and she would fish, and the field where she had seen the angel.

But then, when she finally turned on her side, ready for sleep, she thought, "But it's for Dad's sake, so it's worth it."

And then, "That maypole... what was that rhyme....?

> *"A maypole in the month of May*
> *Is magical — or so they say...."*

And she sighed and shivered at the strong sense of magic, and slept and dreamed all night of maypoles ringed by dancing children, almost as if part of her already knew what was to come, and what strange adventures would befall her and into what secret world she would go, all because of a maypole.

Chapter 2

Aunt Em's was a house of old furniture, embroidered mats and cushions, half drawn curtains and, at times, a thick, funereal silence. This was broken only by the heavy ticking of a grandfather clock that stood in the hall. That tick reached every furthest cranny of the house, it followed Polly even in her dreams. The sampler that hung above the sideboard in the best room observed that *Cleanliness is Next To Godliness*, though it had not, surprisingly enough, been stitched by Aunt Em herself, or even one of her ancestors. She had seen it in the W.I. Bring and Buy, she told them, and been instantly taken by it.

Polly reflected that, if asked, she herself would have associated darkness with dirt, and cleanliness with light, and that it was astonishing that Aunt Em had managed to make cleanliness and dark go hand in hand. Within hours of arriving at Forge Cottage Polly had found herself rhyming, and the rhymes that floated to the surface most were "gloom" and "doom".

Polly's first sight of her aunt had been when the taxi drew up outside the cottage. As the driver and Alice heaved out the luggage, Polly stood staring up at the nearby maypole on the green. It was twice as high as she had imagined it, and in the instant of seeing it, she knew that she had been right. Even now, in broad daylight, bare of ribbons and bright garlands and rings of weaving dancers, it spelled utter and certain magic. She felt her bones melting with it, and went into a trance where she could almost see it circled by dancing children all in white, as she had in her dreams, and hear faint voices singing:

Come lasses and lads
Take leave of your dads
And away to the maypole hie!...

"Oh!" she gasped softly. "You *are* a magic sort of a thing!"

"Polly. *Polly!*"

Polly turned slowly and came out of her dream.

"Say how d'you do to your aunt!" Alice hissed.

Polly turned her gaze, still quite blank, towards the open door of the house.

"So you'll be Polly," said Aunt Em.

"Sticks and stones," Polly thought. "She's got bones like sticks and stones."

Out loud she said, "How d'you do, Aunt Em. I'm glad to meet you."

She was, of course, nothing of the sort. Polly had pictured her aunt in the last few days, but it now became clear she had been far too hopeful. Aunt Em was tall and bony, which might not have been her fault, but her face was sour and her eyes were cold — and that, undoubtedly, was.

"You'd better fetch that luggage inside, if you please," Aunt Em told the taxi driver.

"I daresay he charged you twice over," she told Alice, as the door shut behind him. "They all do."

Polly was surprised to find her aunt so knowledge-able on the subject of taxis. When did she ever ride in one, she wondered? She was later to discover that Aunt Em was an expert on a great number of subjects, from bed-making to weather-forecasting.

"You'll be tired, Alice," she said now. "You'd best go and lie on your bed while I get tea."

"Best — what?"

Alice obviously could not believe her ears. Polly

could remember only a handful of occasions when her mother had taken to her bed in the daytime.

"Lie on your bed. Rest," said Aunt Em. "Do you good."

"But I don't feel like lying down, Em," said poor Alice. "I'm only ever so little tired. I could help you to get the tea."

"That," said Aunt Em, folding her arms across her wrap-around pinny, "is exactly what I don't want, Alice."

"But I *must* help, Em!" cried Alice.

"You can't be waiting on us all hand and foot! And besides —" She broke off, but Polly thought that what she was about to say was that she, Alice Flint, would go clear out of her mind without a job to do. Her inability to waste a single moment was a joke between Polly and Tom at home.

"If ever your mother does run short of summat to do," he would say, "she'll be out there measuring up them pigeons for waistcoats, and baking mincepies for 'em!"

And he was not exactly joking. Alice loved to work, especially with her hands, and as she worked she sang.

"Now look you here, Alice," began Em, "there's one thing to be straightened out between us before we even start. Sit you down and listen, for it must be said."

Alice and Polly both sat down on the extreme edges of their chairs, and listened, and stared up into her face.

"You've come here to stop for a while, and I'm glad to have you," she said. "I'd do as much for anyone, I hope, let alone my own flesh and blood."

"Oh, I *know*, Em!" cried Alice, "and we're —"

"But!" Aunt Em held up a hand. Evidently a tremendous "but" was to follow. "*But* — this is my house. Home. And especially, Alice, it is my kitchen. And that's why I mean to start as I mean to go on. There is only room for one woman in a kitchen, Alice. Once we understand that, I'm sure we shall get along a treat."

"But surely sometimes...?" pleaded Alice. "Just to make a few scones, perhaps, or bread, or —"

Up went the hand again.

"No. The running of this house is up to me, and me alone. I've been here thirty years, near on, and have my own way of doing things. I don't like fuss, and I don't like change."

"No, Em," said Alice weakly.

Polly's heart went out to her cheerful, busy mother — sentenced now, it seemed, to a future of dreary inactivity.

"Does that mean I shan't have to make my bed, Aunt Em?" she inquired sweetly, but with intent to infuriate.

"You'll make your bed," said Aunt Em, "and then I shall look at it. If you don't make it right, then I'll *teach* you to make it right."

"Oh. Thank you." Polly was now as neatly reduced as Alice. The pair of them sat helplessly staring up at Em.

"So," said Aunt Em, closing the matter, "I'll show you to your rooms."

She turned, and they obediently followed.

"Now, these *are* nice," said Alice to Polly, as Aunt Em's footsteps retreated. She was whispering.

"Mine's lovely!" Polly whispered back. "Fancy looking right out at the maypole!"

"And look at the pretty bedspread — all patchwork! D'you know, I half believe I remembered it, from when *I* was your age!"

"Why are we whispering?" asked Polly suddenly in her normal voice. It sounded so loud that they stared pop-eyed at one another for a moment, and then burst into uncontrollable giggles. Alice fetched out her handkerchief and dabbed at her eyes and gasped "Oh dear! Oh dear!" and Polly threw herself down on the bed and stuffed the bedspread into her mouth to smother laughter. Back and forth they rocked until at last Alice started to recover.

"Oh dear! Oh deary me!" she said again, wiping her eyes. "Do be careful with that cover, Polly. Here — use this!"

Polly sat up, dabbing her own streaming eyes.

"If you don't make it right," she gasped, mimicking Aunt Em, "then I'll teach you to make it right!"

"Now give over, Polly, do. You'll set me right off again. Hush!"

Slowly their mirth subsided.

"Anyway, it *is* nice," Alice said, looking about her. "Plain white walls and nice old beams — don't you like them beams? And I've got a nice view, as well. It is *prettier* here, Polly, than at home. That you must admit."

"Come and have another look at my room."

Back they went over the landing and into the little room overlooking the village green.

"Oh, it is lovely." exclaimed Alice.

"We're ever so lucky, you know, Polly. When you think of the trouble we're in, with Tom... and then... oh..." she broke off, now nearer to tears than giggles. "We must try to fit in, Polly. You will try, won't you? Your aunt means well, I do know that. It's a big upset, us all coming into her house after all those

29

years on her own. I can understand that. Do try, there's a good girl."

"Yes, Mam."

But Polly was not listening at all. She was looking out on to the green and at that towering maypole and again catching glimpses and hearing snatches of song, and thinking, "There's a whole other world out there, I know there is. Side by side with this, there's a secret world, and I'm going to find it, I am!"

She and Alice unpacked their things. They enjoyed putting their neatly laundered clothes into the empty (but nonetheless mothballed) drawers. Polly set a selection of her favourite toys and pictures about the room, and looked about with satisfaction.

"It *does* seem like home, a bit," she decided.

Then came Aunt Em's call from the foot of the stairs and Polly and Alice dutifully descended, daring each other to giggle.

The three of them sat around the gateleg table with its embroidered linen cloth and plates of ham salad. Aunt Em poured thick brown tea from a teapot dressed in a green woolly waistcoat, and urged her visitors to eat up.

"That's right!" she exclaimed as Alice put down her knife and fork. "That's what I like to see, a nice clean plate."

"That's what you used to say when we were little. When *I* was little."

Aunt Em seemed temporarily taken aback.

"Did I? Well, fancy. Come along, Polly, finish up. Then we can go on to the trifle."

"I don't think I can eat any more, Aunt Em," Polly said.

"It'll be all the excitement," said Alice swiftly. "She's usually ever such a good little eater."

"There's no need for her to have the trifle — it's the one I used to make — your favourite, Alice. But she's to finish what she's got on her plate. You shouldn't take what you can't eat."

"But the salad was already laid out on the plate!" protested Polly.

Aunt Em was floored for a moment by this truth.

"Now stop fussing," she said, "and eat up!"

Polly speared a piece of pinkish, rubbery ham and looked at it.

"Ugh!" she thought, "I'll be sick!" And then, "Bet Aunt *Em* don't eat what she don't want!"

She put the fork down again.

"I can't," she said. "I'm sorry."

Alice swiftly reached for Polly's plate, scraped its contents on to her own, and stacked them. Aunt Em eyed this manoeuvre with patent disapproval.

"I hope you know what you're encouraging, Alice."

Polly sat there, listening to the ruthless ticking of the clock in the hall, and longing for bedtime.

"She *is* kind," said Alice to Polly later, as she saw her to bed for the first time in this strange place. "That trifle of hers always was my favourite — and she'd remembered it all these years! D'you know, I feel half guilty now that we haven't seen more of her. I mean, it must be lonely for her here on her own."

"I think she likes it," said Polly.

"Likes what?"

"Being alone. I think we're going to be a bother to her."

"Now don't say that!" cried Alice in consternation. "We shall be here for weeks and weeks — perhaps months and months!"

"I'm only saying what I think, Mam," Polly said. "Dad says I should always say what I think. And oh, tomorrow he'll be here! Oh — won't he think it wonderful, after hospital."

"Your father," said Alice slowly, "inclines to see everything wonderful, if he can. Even when he's laid flat and can't stir a step. Sees everything wonderful."

"Oh, I know, Mam!" and now they clung together in tears as before they had clung in helpless laughter, and eyes had to be dried again.

"Sleep well, then," Alice said. She stood by the window. "It is nice for you, this view. Em says that maypole's one of the oldest in England. Been there centuries, she says."

"Yes," said Polly, and not a word more. She knew — or felt — more about that maypole already than ever Aunt Em could tell her, but kept her lips tightly buttoned.

"My secret," she thought. "Mine."

"Ah well!" Alice drew both curtains together at once. "Tomorrow's another day..."

Polly giggled weakly.

"Oh Mam, you are daft. Of course tomorrow's another day!"

"Just a manner of speaking," said Alice. "And like you, Polly Flint, to take me up on it. Goodnight."

She bent to kiss her and Polly could smell her hair, newly washed last night for this great adventure, and on an impulse threw up her arms and hugged her.

"Goodnight! I *like* it here, I do."

"Little lamb." Alice had not called her this for ages. "Good girl. God bless."

And then she was gone. Gone to cry for a while in her own room, Polly guessed, before going down again to spend the evening with Aunt Em. And she wept a little herself for her brave mother, who overnight had left her own home and become a visitor in a strange place, all her roots pulled up.

"But it's all for a *reason!*" Polly told herself fiercely. "Dad will get better, he will, he will!"

And then, after a time, she knelt up on her bed and parted the curtains. There it still was in the twilight, the green and its maypole. And for the first time she noticed, right opposite, The Red Lion, brightly lit and with voices floating out into the quiet evening.

"Oh!" she said softly to the maypole. "I know that you and I are to meet. I know that you have a secret, and I shall find it."

She was about to let the curtains fall, and lie back again, when she saw a movement. It was a figure lit from behind by the lights of the inn, and with a long shadow falling almost to the foot of the maypole. What she saw was a gigantic shadow with its arms raised.

"Strange..." thought Polly. "What it reminds me of, is a magician making a spell."

She stared and stared, but in the end the pattern made by the pole and the giant shadow and the figure itself went into a kind of blur. She blinked and rubbed at her eyes, and when she looked again, the pattern had dissolved. All she saw was the maypole, and beyond it a tall shadowy figure moving away and towards the inn. She shook her head, and sank back on to the pillows.

Next day, Tom was to be brought.

"You'd best not go far," Alice told Polly, who was itching to explore her new world. "Not if you want to be here when he comes."

Polly wandered out into the sunlight and on to the

dewy green to greet her maypole — for already she thought of it as hers. It had been there centuries, she thought, and knew a thousand secrets.

"Who're you?"

Polly turned and saw that the voice belonged to a boy of about her own age.

"Who're you?" she countered.

"You're new here," he said. "I'm not. Everybody knows who I am. Did you come out of old hag Ridler's house?"

"My aunt Em lives there," said Polly, "and she is *not* a hag."

"Stopping with her, are you?"

"I might be." Polly had hoped to make friends in her new world, but knew already that this boy would not be one of them.

"Pity you, then," he said. "Old hag!"

She began to walk away, annoyed that he had interrupted her conversation with the maypole. At the other side of the green she saw a man sitting on a bench outside the Red Lion. He was looking straight at her.

"Morning!" he called.

"Good morning," Polly replied, and he made a gesture beckoning her to cross over to him, and unthinkingly she obeyed.

"Well, now," he said, "you'll be new."

Polly thought to herself, "Well, now, you'll be old!"

His face was mapped with a thousand lines, and browned by wind and weather. One hand curved over a gnarled stick, the other lay on his knee like a piece of bark. Polly looked right into his bright and wicked eyes.

"I'm Polly Flint," she told him.

"Well, now..."

"And I'm stopping with my Aunt Em. Miss Ridler, over the road."

"Emily Ridler, is it," he murmured. "And shall you be stopping long, Polly Flint?"

"Could be," said Polly. "It depends. My father's poorly, you see."

"All summer?"

"I should think all summer," she replied, and wondered why he should ask.

"You'll be here for the May Dancing."

"Oh, I shall! I'm longing for it!"

"They'll deck that pole with garlands," he said. "Garlands, and brave ribbons, and dance the old dances..."

A little silence fell. Polly cast round for something to say to this strange man. But it was he who spoke first.

"Have they told you?" His voice was lowered now, he was speaking of secrets to be told.

"Told me? What?"

"Of the lost village..."

Polly felt a little cold thrill at the nape of her neck. Slowly, her eyes locked to his, she shook her head.

"Aaaah!" He let out a long breath. "They not all believe it, see. They think it's nobbut a tale to tell by the fireside. But me, I know it to be true. Tell you, shall I?"

Slowly Polly nodded.

"Hundreds of years ago, hundreds and hundreds, there was a village standing where we are now... right here, on this very spot..."

"What can he mean?" Polly wondered. "There still is a village."

"And the name of that village," he went on, "was Grimstone. And it wasn't very big — oh no, not at all,

35

and in fact it had hardly the number of children it needed to dance the May Dances."

There was a silence.

"And then —" he paused, "and then — it vanished."

Polly swallowed hard.

"Vanished?" Her voice came out very high and thin.

"It vanished — right off the face of the earth! Or rather — as some believe — was swallowed right *into* the earth! What do you say to that?"

Polly shook her head dumbly. He was watching her with something like triumph.

"Legend goes," he went on, "that if you kneel and put your ear to the ground on Christmas Day, you can hear the church bells still, ringing away down there."

Again she shook her head and stared into his eyes.

"Away down there — under all this —" he waved a long arm about him — "the church bells ringing! That's what the legend says. What I say," he leaned towards her again, his voice down almost to a whisper, "is that you can hear them bells *any* Sabbath, if you will."

"Really hear them? Through the ground?"

"Lay your ear to the turf and listen," he said. "You'll hear 'em ringing, sweet and true. And that ain't all..."

"What?"

"Ah... signs for those with ears to hear and eyes to see. Voices. Flitting shapes and shadows... faint music... reflections...."

"Reflections?"

"In the lake. You get by that lake, and you'll be but a fingertip away. Water... Water always finds its own level..."

"You *mean*," said Polly Flint, deciding to state the case in her own words, since he was so full of enigma and glancing meanings, "you mean, that there's a village down there *still*?"

"I say," he replied, "that when the earth opened to swallow it up, in that very instant — it slipped the net of time!"

"Slipped the net of time..." Polly pondered. "Still there, then. But if it *is* still there, where...?"

"Polly! Polly!"

It was Alice, calling from beyond the green.

"Come on back, will you? I want you!"

"Yes, Mam!" she called back, and then told him, "My mother. I'll have to go. But thank you for telling me the story. Goodbye!"

And she was off, running, not out of any particular desire to please Alice, but because she had had as much magic as she could stand, for the time being.

It turned out that the stranger was the reason for her being called back. Aunt Em had spotted them from a window as she took down some curtains.

"You keep away from that Old Mazy," she said. "Same as everybody else."

"Is that his name? Old Mazy?"

"What we call him. Mazed in the head, of course."

"How long has he lived here?" Polly was not quite sure what she hoped to hear — centuries, perhaps?

"Lived? He don't *live* here, for a good job. Just turns up, round about this time of year. Stops a few weeks, then gone again till next year. You let him well alone, d'you hear me?"

"He told me a story," Polly said. "About a village that vanished. That was swallowed, right into the earth, in the twinkling of an eye — houses, fields, people and all! Is it *true*?"

37

"Now what do *you* think!" Aunt Em sounded disgusted. She was not a believer in magic, nor even mysteries. "Now — from under my feet, if you please!"

She made a sweeping movement with a long cobweb brush, seriously endangering a potted fern, and Polly noticed that she was wearing a scarf swathed turban-wise around her head.

"To sweep the cobwebs out of the sky!" thought Polly, and almost giggled.

"Your aunt's having a spring clean," said Alice, somewhat desperately. She was pulling some kind of face at Polly over Aunt Em's shoulder.

"A thorough spring clean," affirmed Aunt Em, with grim satisfaction.

"But — Dad's coming!"

"Room already done," she said. "Ready and waiting."

"But —"

Alice's grimace intensified, and Polly stopped short.

"Can I help?" she asked, half-heartedly.

Neither Alice nor Polly could help, it seemed. Aunt Em alone could carry out the attack. She alone knew the crevices where dust could gather, spiders lurk. She alone knew why she should pick this particular day, out of three hundred and sixty-four others, to tackle the enemy — the very day Tom was to come.

Alice thought she could guess.

"It's to show us all it's *her* house," she explained to Polly later. "It must seem like — well, like a kind of threat, us all coming. As if we were invaders. She's just keeping her end up, that's all."

"This house is too clean already," Polly said, and Alice laughed. And then the door knocker banged, and it was Tom, coming home at last — or at least, to a kind of home.

He was installed in a big high bed specially put up in a downstairs room, and when the men had gone away, Polly ran in to see him there.

"Oh Dad, Dad!" She bent to kiss him, and then stood back, and then laughed. "Oh, it does seem funny! You should see yourself!"

"Oh yes," said Tom. "Laughing at me now, are you?"

"It's just that — well, all this —" sweeping her arm to indicate the room which contained, besides Tom's bed, an old-fashioned sofa and chairs, a cabinet of china, numerous covers and cushions and gilt-framed pictures, and even an old upright piano. "And Dad — you should just see what's hanging over your head!"

Obligingly he rolled up his eyes towards the stitched sampler in its mahogany frame.

"Sampler, I can see that. No — can't read it. Go on — tell."

"Cleanliness is next to Godliness!"

They both laughed.

From where he lay, Tom could see the top part of the maypole with its golden weathercock.

"It's magic, Dad," Polly told him, "so you'd best keep your eye on it. And you'll never guess what *else*!"

And she told him about Old Mazy, and the legend of the vanished village.

"And then he said, 'It slipped the net of time.' What does it mean, Dad?"

"I don't know," Tom admitted at last. "But it's surely a beautiful picture it makes in your head. Beautiful."

"You can lie there and think about it," Polly told

him, "and maybe write a rhyme about it. And me —
I'll go and find that village, if it's there!"

"That's my lass!" Tom said. "Like it here, do you?"

Polly shook her head.

"Not yet," she said. "But I expect I shall, in the
end. Especially now you've come. But I just wish
Aunt Em wasn't so *clean*."

"That her banging away out there, is it?"

"Spring cleaning!" said Polly scornfully. "This
house'll vanish, if she doesn't watch out. Swept clear
away, it'll be!"

"Ah well. Her house, remember. You've got to let
her be queen in her own kingdom, Polly."

Aunt Em was certainly being as bossy as any
queen. And wherever Polly turned to tuck herself
away, she found herself under Aunt Em's feet. There
were regular cries of "Polly — don't!" from Alice,
who sat frantically knitting even though summer
was coming, and kept dropping stitches in her fre-
quent moves from place to place to be out of her sister's way.

Straight after dinner Polly left the house. She ran
straight past the maypole and on toward Rufford
Park.

"There's plenty to see there," Aunt Em had said,
"but watch out for the lake, and don't get into any
mischief."

"If I could *think* of any mischief, I'd get up to it, all
right," she thought as she ran. "I would, for certain
definite."

She slowed as she saw the ford ahead, a shallow
stream crossing the road. She stepped to its edge.
What she really wanted was to paddle over, though
she knew there was no need. She saw the little footbridge Aunt Em had told her about. She looked

toward the left, and saw the sun glancing through the leaves and striking spears of light into the water. The stream was shallow, clear in the sunlight, and thickly green in the shade.

"Tadpoles," thought Polly longingly. "Minnows, tiddlers, sticklebacks and — wheee!"

She was drenched from head from head to foot with icy water. She turned and glared after the retreating car. The grinning face of a boy looked back from the rear window.

"And mustard tarts to you, too!" she screamed. She shook herself and looked down at her splattered front.

"Found some mischief to get into, I s'pose," she thought. "Only good thing about it."

Over the footbridge she went, and towards a little clearing, where she hesitated. Little paths ran away through the trees on all sides. Which to take? Birds whistled about her and she listened, already approving the place, pleased with the feel of it.

"Left," she decided, for no real reason, and took that path, and the next minute was looking out over a wide, shining lake and was astonished by the suddenness of it.

"Oh!" she gasped. "Oh moon and stars! Ain't it just..."

She was dumbstruck. She stood and took it all in. It was the widest stretch of water she had ever seen — inland water, not counting the sea. There was not another person in sight. Even the sky seemed bigger and emptier than usual.

"And birds!" she exclaimed. "And ducks, and geese and — things!"

Flotillas of them there were, some swimming or gliding, others stalking the wooden planks of a kind

41

of platform, or deck, at the near end of the lake.

Polly Flint, who knew what she liked when she saw it, was almost mad with delight. She flung out her arms, and cried,

"*My* kingdom! This is my kingdom, and I am the queen!"

She ran forward and the birds all went into storm and the ducks came swimming swiftly towards her as if to a summons, and quacked in chorus, as if to greet her. (They were expecting bread to be thrown, but Polly was not to know that.)

"They heard!" she gasped, hardly able to believe it herself, though she was very good at believing in almost anything.

She marched on then through her new kingdom, taking it all in and bestowing names, left and right. She passed an island, with a low arched tunnel passing right under it.

"You are the Secret Tunnel!" she proclaimed.

She paused to regard a passing family of ducks.

"Swans, royal birds should be, really," she thought. "But I don't care. I'm the queen, and you are my royal ducks!"

They swam on as carelessly as ducks do in the early spring when the air is warm and the water calm.

She came to a smaller pool, where silver birches on the far side went reaching down into the green depths.

"You are the Silver Pool!" she cried. "I am queen, and I name you — Silver Pool!"

And then, quite suddenly, she was aware of echoes, of whisperings, of hints, inklings, reflections. And she heard again the words of Old Mazy:

"Water always finds its own level..."

Polly Flint, feeling herself but a fingertip away from magic, shivered.

Chapter 3

And so from that time onward Polly Flint began to live in two separate worlds. There was the world of every day, of clocks ticking and rain falling and the polish-smelling kingdom of Aunt Em. And there was her own, secret world, where she reigned over her own kingdom and even time seemed to stand still for her.

The very next day she returned to the lake, and this time she went all the way round it, counting the little overgrown islands, giving names to the smaller pools that led off on the further side. And as she walked, it seemed to her that now and again, faintly, she heard children's voices, and laughter. Then she would stop and listen intently, but always was left with the feeling that she *might* have heard something — or she might not.

She told Tom about her kingdom. She described to him the different birds, the pool with the reflection of five silver birches, the curious arched tunnel that went under one of the islands.

"I can see it as clear as with my own eyes," he told her.

"And one day you'll see it for yourself," said Polly. "*And* I bet there's fish in there!"

Then she went for the first time to the village school, and came running home for dinner with her news.

"They're practising the May Dances!" she cried, "and I can't join in!"

"Now that is a shame," said Alice, "you being so keen on the maypole, and all."

43

"It's not fair! It's not fair!"

"Only to be expected," said Aunt Em. "Very complicated, them dances. I've seen them. In and out and up and down, and plaiting the ribbons as they go. Takes *months* to learn them, I daresay."

"And another thing!" cried Polly. "They're not *doing* it on May Day! May Day's on Tuesday, and they're doing it on the Saturday after."

"Always do," said Aunt Em infuriatingly. "Got to do it on a Saturday, so that folk can come and watch. No use doing dances for the birds."

"It *is*!" Polly almost screamed. "You don't understand! It's magic! You have to do it at the break of day, on May Day."

"I never heard such rubbish," said Aunt Em. "And lower your voice, if you please. Fine audience they'd get at crack of dawn!"

"But it isn't *meant* for an audience!"

Polly despaired of making them understand. Those dances, she well knew, should be danced in the mysterious half-light of dawn, barefoot in the dew wet grass. They should be danced solemnly, a celebration of life, of all greenness and growth, of all the mystery of the world.

But she did not tell them this. Nor did she tell them of her secret knowledge that the maypole was the key to another even greater mystery, and another world.

"And there's another thing," she contented herself with saying, "they don't even have a May Queen!"

"And I suppose you were fancying yourself as that!" said Aunt Em waspishly.

"They have a *gypsy* king and queen! Whoever heard of *that*?"

"Always have." Aunt Em was maddeningly in the

know. "It's a tradition, round here. There's always been a boy and a girl picked, gypsy king and queen."

Polly eyed her coldly.

"Thinks she knows it all," she thought. "And she don't know *owt*!"

From that moment she decided that she would celebrate her own May Day. Over the next few days she hatched her plan. She would see May in on her own. She would set her alarm clock for five o'clock, and go out on to the green and herself dance round the maypole.

"No-one'll see me," she thought. "no-one about, that early."

And this secret scheme took her happily through the next few days. She now watched the other children practising their steps, without in the least wanting to join in. She watched only to learn some of the steps that she might copy. Then she would run to the lake and practise them there. She wove the steps back and forth and round a silver birch that she had cast as pole.

She never saw anyone else there until the last evening in April. She was practising her steps, and humming "Polly Put the Kettle On", because this was one of the tunes the children danced to, in a dance called "The Gypsy's Tent". All at once, as she skipped and bobbed, she was again aware of magic at work.

"My name," she thought. "My very own name — and the main dance! Must mean something, that must!"

Breathless she came to a halt, and bowed to her invisible partner. Then, above the sound of her own breathing she heard a rustling and snapping of twigs, and looked into the copse beyond and saw a figure go

45

striding by. It was there and gone in a trice, hidden by the trees, but Polly saw it for long enough to know that this was no ordinary visitor, come to feed the birds or walk the dog.

The man (for she saw that it was a man) went with long bounding strides — scissoring through the bracken — and yet there was a curious dreamlike slowness to his movements, as in a film show in slow motion. He might have been treading on air. And raised in his right arm was a long rod and a — "*Net*?" Polly shook her head to settle it. Who would go striding through the woods at evening with a huge net, as if to catch some mysterious quarry?

"Not for butterflies," she thought, "nor even birds. Much too big." Again she shook her head.

"Must've dreamed it," she thought. "All that twizzling."

On this occasion, even Polly Flint herself could not believe her own eyes.

She wandered home in the blue steepling shadows and from time to time she shivered. It was the eve of May Day, and already magic was abroad in the air. The grass was sprinkled with daisies, half closed now.

"'Tisn't spring till you can plant your foot on twelve daisies," she thought dreamily. "That's what Mam says. *Tomorrow* it'll be spring!"

And the thought came to her that she would make a chaplet of daisies to wear on her head next day. She sat straight down on the cold grass and began to pick and thread them.

"I shall wear this," she thought, "and I shall keep my nightie on — at any rate it's white, and long, and near the proper thing!"

A few minutes, and the thing was done. She tried the garland for size, nodded, satisfied, and started again

46

for home. She turned the corner on to the green.

"It's Polly Flint!" she heard. "Oooh — look at that!"

Davey Cole was there with his friends, and she realised too late why they were pointing and laughing. She snatched the daisy chain from her head and began to run.

"Wake me early, mother dear," they chanted after her, "for I'm to be Queen of the May!" and again, "Wake me early, Mother dear, for I'm to be Queen of the May!"

She dashed into the house and slammed the door behind her.

"Polly — *don't*!" she heard Alice's voice. "Come along here, I want you."

She was knitting, somewhat desperately, as usual. Aunt Em was embroidering yet another cloth.

"I don't like doors slammed," she observed. "Not in this house, thank you."

"Do remember, Polly," begged Alice.

"I'm sorry," said Polly, but only for her mother's sake.

"What's that you've got?" Alice asked.

Polly opened up her palm.

"Oh — a daisy chain!"

"Those that've got time to stitch daisies," remarked Aunt Em, "could as well be stitching something useful."

"What I should really like," thought Polly, "would be to stitch your mouth up, for good and all!"

"Go and say goodnight to your father," said Alice. "You're late. We were beginning to wonder. I'll bring you up some milk."

Polly gladly went out and across the passage and past the dictatorial clock to where Tom lay, quite still

47

in the half light.

"Asleep, Dad?" she whispered.

"Not asleep," came the answer, "but dreaming."

"Flying, were you?"

"Aye. Flying." He drew a long breath, a sigh.

"Just come to say goodnight. Been down by the lake. All silver it was, when I left. Wish you could've seen it."

A sudden thought struck her.

"Why not? Dad, it's May Day tomorrow!"

"And so it is, Poll," he said.

"And I just *wonder*," she went on swiftly, "if, with it being a magic sort of a time — you know, like Midsummer Eve or Hallowe'en, and that — why not — why not make a *wish*?"

"A wish... why, there's never any harm in wishing, Poll."

"I know that. I spend half my *life* wishing. What I mean is, it might be one of the times when wishes actually come true!"

"It might, at that," he agreed. "Try, shall we?"

"Oh let's, Dad! But neither of us to tell, for fear it breaks the spell!"

She laughed.

"Rhymed without even meaning to! But neither of us to tell, for fear it breaks the spell!"

She leant over the bed to kiss him, and was half tempted to tell him her secret. But this was so private a thing that not even Tom could know.

"Afterwards," she thought. "Perhaps."

Then she went up, set her alarm clock for five o'clock and put it just under the bed, with the daisy chain. She fetched out her long white nightdress instead of the one that was under her pillow. That one was not at all suitable for a serious occasion, being of bright pink with rabbits and buttercups right across the chest. When Alice came up to say goodnight Polly pulled the bedclothes up to her chin, in case the exchange was noticed, and remarked upon.

And when the curtains were drawn and Alice gone, Polly turned on her side and fell asleep almost straight away, and she slept all night without a single dream, as if she knew that the dreams were yet to come.

And so the night passed swiftly, as dreamless nights do, and when the alarm rang Polly was wide awake in the instant. She stretched out a hand to stop the bell and sat up and stared at the curtains, where only the faintest light seemed to show. She knelt on the bed and parted them.

There lay the green, the cottages, the church tower beyond, all strangely bleached of colour and robbed of outline in the dawn half-light. The sky itself was blank and grey with not a hint or tinge of the coming sunrise. But the sunrise was certain, that Polly did know — and she raised her arm in salute to the maypole before dropping the curtains again. It stood intent, as if it were waiting. Polly shivered. Her teeth started to chatter.

Softly she opened the door of the room, and stole tiptoe down the telltale stairs. The grandfather clock was relentlessly telling the time — tick tock tick tock. There was a chink of chain, the turn of a key — and Polly was out.

She stood and looked about her, all alone in that vast dawn hush. Far away she heard a cock crow, and the thought crossed her mind that it might come from the farm beyond the inn, or it might be calling from some hidden stack in the buried village of

49

Grimstone down below.

And no sooner had she thought this, than she heard faint voices singing, and strange music. The voices were those of children, and all the children of Wellow, Polly well knew, were still fast in their beds and sleeping. She stared at the greyish, dewed green, and half expected it to open up under her eyes. Now the voices were closer. They were singing a song that she knew well.

> *"Come lasses and lads*
> *Take leave of your dads*
> *And away to the maypole hie!"*

"They're coming! They're dancing the Spider's Web!"

Polly's heart thudded hard. She strained into that milky half light and saw shapes making themselves, shadows blossoming. The May Dancers were coming, they were slipping into the upper world, running free in time!

At first they were merely faint and ghostly, and then they took on a sepia tinge as in an old print, and she saw that the girls wore dresses all of white and garlands on their heads, and each was weaving a pattern; heel and toe they went about the boys, who stood staring straight ahead and motionless as statues. And all the while the bright ribbon that now miraculously crowned the pole was crissing and crossing to form the mazy pattern of a spider's web.

Polly started forward. Her bare feet were heedless of the icy dew.

Now a troop of tiny children ran forward under the ribbons with squeals of delight, and the fiddles struck up a different tune, and another dance began.

Polly's thoughts were very strange and slow.

"They are all in the Spider's Web," she thought. "Web... net... slipped the net of time..."

All the time the dawn was inexorably breaking and the scene was lit with a thin wash of gold. The net of streamers glowed and the grass was all at once on fire and dazzling. And as Polly Flint stood all alone stock-still and staring, she saw now that the dancers had no shadows!

She shut her eyes and shook her head, stunned.

And then they fled. They went, not running, but dancing their way out of time again. The bright figures dissolved, first to shadows, then to air. The music dwindled to a pale echo.

Silence. The sun struck fire from dew and leaf and blade. Dumbstruck, Polly Flint wheeled about for hint or sign, and saw none. Slowly she advanced and looked down at the turf as she went. The dew lay innocent and undisturbed where lately dancers went. Polly sighed a deep sigh and half turned away and then turned back and saw — footprints!

"Oh!" gasped Polly Flint. "Oh my moon and stars!"

She peered and saw a narrow darkened streak running through the silver. She started to follow it, planting her own feet exactly on the line, heel to toe. She did not explain to herself why she did this. It simply seemed to be at the same time a very magic and very natural thing to do. She might even have half hoped that she, too, would be sent reeling out of time.

At any rate she solemnly trod that teasing line, watching her own feet go heel to toe with ritual care. She had not the least idea what she hoped to see, but it was certainly not the abrupt end of the trail where grass met tarmac, and she let out a cry of disap-

51

pointment. Left and right she scanned the road, but knew as she did so that the scent was lost. She turned and looked back over the deserted green.

"I shouldn't have *trod* it," she thought, dismayed. "Now all I can see are *my* footsteps."

It even fleetingly crossed her mind that she might not have seen human footprints in the first place, that she might have seen only what she wanted to see, and had been following the harmless path of a cat, or rabbit.

Slowly and thoughtfully Polly Flint followed her own path back toward home.

That evening, as she was walking along one of the woodland paths, watching the sun shaft down to light the silver stems of the birches, and tarnish the brilliant green of the new bracken, she heard, beyond the whistling of birds, clear echoing laughter. She stopped and listened, and this time it did not fade, and she glanced half fearfully about her.

"Oh my!" she thought. "Hold fast, Polly! There is someone there!"

On impulse she dropped to her knees.

"If there is," she thought, "I'll see them before they see me!"

The echoing voices were all around her, it seemed at first, but gradually the hollowness faded and she heard them, quite distinctly, to her left. Without thinking she jumped back on to her feet, and there they were. She saw them plainly, a boy and a girl, about her own age, wading knee high in the bracken.

She cried, "Oh!" out loud, and clapped her hand to her mouth as the pair stopped dead still and looked toward her. Her eyes met theirs for a few seconds, all three of them stood frozen, and then they were off, darting swiftly between the trees and soon cut off from sight behind the foliage. Polly was too startled to give chase until it was too late. She made her way to the spot where they had disappeared. Nothing. No voices, no laughter, not even the rustle of grass or fern or telltale snap of a twig.

"Hello!" she called. And then again, "Hello!"

Only the faint roar of traffic from the road beyond, and the evening whistling of birds.

Very slowly Polly turned and retraced her steps. She did not put into words the reason why she did not go further into the woods. She did not admit that she was afraid. As she went, she tried to recall that brief sighting.

"The strangest thing is..." she thought, "...no, I must be wrong. Can't have seen that...."

And yet at the back of her mind she was perfectly certain that as they ran she had seen that the girl had been holding something round, and to Polly it had looked like —

"A tambourine!" she said out loud.

Her mistake was to tell about what had happened.

"I saw a boy and a girl in the woods just now. And would you believe, the girl was wearing a *bonnet*?"

"Oh yes?" said Alice. "Was your eyes open or shut at the time?"

"And holding a tambourine," went on Polly. "It was the queerest thing. And I even thought I heard it jangle." Alice shook her head.

"Just one of her fancies," she explained to Aunt Em. "Thinks she sees things. Bit of a dreamer, like her father."

"I wasn't dreaming! It was real!"

"Real to you, I daresay," said Alice. "But what anyone else would call daydreams."

Polly was furious.

53

"How do you know what's real and what's not? How do you know I'm not dreaming *you* — 'cos I saw those two as plain as I see you! How d'you know *you're* not dreams? Just you tell me that!"

She stared back at their open-mouthed faces, pushed back her chair and fled. She slammed the door behind her.

"Polly — don't!" came Alice's voice from the other side.

Polly wandered away from the house, kicking at the turf of the green, glaring at her feet.

"That settles it!" she thought. "Once for all. Never believe anything I say, they don't!"

She became aware of a long shadow moving ahead, and raised her eyes. She was looking straight into the low sun and had to shield her eyes with a hand, and at first saw only an outline, long and lank and moving with a curious loping stride, as if perpetually tumbling forward. Then the silhouette resolved itself into a person, and that person was Old Mazy. She had not thought him so tall.

"Evening!" she called, heedless of Aunt Em's warning, indeed, in deliberate defiance of it.

He stopped and turned.

"Why, good evening," he replied.

Polly was seized by an urge to tell him what she had seen.

"He'll believe me," she thought.

"You know what you were telling me the other day," she began. "About the vanished village, and about the..."

She did not quite know how to put it.

"Go on," he said. "You've seen something, then. Seen? Heard?"

She nodded. He moved closer.

54

"Going to tell, are you?" he said softly.

"Saw," she said. "Today. In the wood by the lake."

"Ah. By the lake."

"I think — I think I'd heard them before. Kind of echoing. But today they came nearer, and they didn't echo..."

"Slipped the net of time," he murmured, as though to himself.

"It was a boy and a girl," she went on with a rush. She had started to tell, and now must finish, get it over with. "And they saw me as well, and then they ran off, and —"

"And?" he prompted.

"Something that stuck in my mind. Something I noticed when they ran. They were holding something, both of them, and the girl — she had a tambourine, I'm sure she had!"

He did look at her now.

"Time gypsies," he said at last.

"Time gypsies?"

"Wanderers," he said. "Not like ordinary gypsies, from place to place. From time to time."

A car went by just then and Polly shook herself, as if awakening from a sleep. Her eyes travelled from the moving car to Old Mazy's face and then to the maypole.

"Not a May Queen," she said slowly. "A gypsy king and queen... of course..."

She looked back at him. She was not sure that she liked him, though she wanted to, to spite her aunt. He wore a curious expression of satisfaction, even gloating.

"Shall you listen?" he asked her suddenly. "Shall you?"

"Listen?"

"For the bells!"

"Ah! Yes, yes, I shall!"

And she did, too. It was not an easy matter. Polly supposed that the church bells of Grimstone away down below would ring at the same time as those of the church above. It seemed likely. She, Alice and Aunt Em set off to the church over the green.

Just as they reached the porch Polly nudged Alice, and whispered, "Forgotten my hanky! Back in a minute!" She darted away. She had already decided where to put her ear to the ground. The best place of all would be by the maypole, she was sure of that, because that was where the magic seemed to gather. But she did not wish to be seen, and so she went swiftly round to the far side of the church.

She was quite alone among the leaning tombstones. She hesitated. Was it really possible that away down there under that innocent turf there was a village snatched out of time? Were there cottages with high hollyhocks and chimneys with smoke rising and smells of dinner wafting through open doors? Was there really a church down there, with weathercock turning in timeless winds and bells ringing out at this very moment, while the people came walking in their Sunday best?

"Only one way to find out," she thought. "Nothing to be scared of, either. Wish my heart would stop banging!"

She dropped to her knees. She could see every blade of grass distinct and separate and the smell was strong and green. Above her the church bells tumbled in the tower. But was there an answer from below, were bells ringing far away down and centuries ago? She strained to catch that peal, because she was certain of it, and certain, too, that she was meant to hear. Now her ear was right to the ground and her heart lurched. She heard them! Faint and sweet she heard those other bells in that other place ringing out from who knew what wild acres lost in time and space?

She listened in a dream and her head was filled with bells, and when they stopped, abruptly, the sudden quiet was huge. She let out a long, shuddering breath and raised herself slowly. So dizzied was she, that at first she forgot that she was out here, in the graveyard, but her mother and Aunt Em would be nudging one another and fidgeting in their pew. It was only the singing that roused her:

> *Morning has broken*
> *Like the first morning,*
> *Blackbird has spoken*
> *Like the first bird...*

"Oooh!" she gave a little shriek. "First hymn! Oooh!"

She began to stumble silly-kneed back round the church and went almost headlong into Davey Cole and shrieked again with surprise.

He laughed right in her face.

"Daft thing!" he told her. "*I* saw you! Wait till I tell 'em!"

"You shut up!" she hissed, keeping her voice churchy as if she were already inside. "You just shut up — and get out of my road!"

She tilted her chin and marched on, but Davey Cole's foot went out and next minute Polly was flat on her face, down in the daisies again. When she had picked herself up he was half way over the green, and she dared not shout after him, as she wanted to. She looked ruefully down and saw that the front of her dress was damp and stained, and hoped that the others would be too busy praying to notice.

It was roast lamb for dinner. This was Polly's favourite and perhaps that was why they decided it would be a good time to tell her. The three of them sat round the table and Tom's door was left open so that he could join in the talking. Polly felt very light and elated. She hugged to herself the sound, the secret sound, of those faraway-down bells.

"Could hear the singing from where I am!" Tom called through. "You did very nicely."

"We were short of a baritone, I thought!" called back Alice smartly.

"Are you going to tell," asked Aunt Em, "or aren't you?"

"What?" asked Polly instantly.

"You tell her, love," came Tom's voice.

"*What*?" demanded Polly again.

"It's about Tom," Alice began. "You see, he won't be stopping here as long as we thought."

"It's *good* news!" Tom roared.

"*What*?" Polly was desperate.

"Me and your Dad are leaving in a day or two, Polly," said Alice. "But you'll be stopping on a bit, with your aunt."

Polly stared.

"Why?"

"He's going to another hospital," Alice told her. "A special one, down in the south. And they think..." her voice shook a little, and Polly saw that her cheeks were brightly flushed, "they think that they might make him better!

"*Will* make me better!" came Tom's roar. "*Will*!"

Polly was torn between delight and despair. Was her father *really* to walk again — and did she really

58

have to stop alone with Aunt Em?

"What do you say to that?" Tom's voice demanded.

Polly flung down her knife and fork and rushed out of the room and over the passage to where he lay. His plate of roast lamb was balanced on his chest and a napkin tucked under his chin.

"Oh Dad!" She was both laughing and crying. "Oh Dad! It's wonderful."

The most important part of the news *was* about him.

"Right way up again," he said. "What do you say to that?"

And for once, Polly Flint could think of nothing to say at all.

Later, Alice said, "I'm sorry, love, I really am. That you'll be left."

"That's all right, Mam," Polly lied.

"She'll maybe soften up a bit, when we're gone," said Alice — meaning Em.

"Yes," said Polly bleakly. Then, "Oh, Mam, *why* did I have to be an only?"

"Now, Polly, *don't*." said Alice. "We've been through all that, hundreds of times."

"If only I had just one other person — just one brother or one sister — or even a baby — or even a *grandma*!"

"You'd not necessarily be any better off at all," said Alice firmly. "You look at Em and me!"

"That's different," said Polly.

"That isn't different at all," replied Alice. "You'd be fighting cat and dog from morning till night. And anyhow, you know it wasn't to be."

Polly wished then that she had kept quiet. She knew very well that Tom and Alice had wanted a houseful of children. But she was scared of the silence that would surely fall when the front door shut behind her mother and father.

And when that time came, only two days later, the silence did fall. Tick-tick-tick-tock — the grandfather clock in the hall came into its own, and it seemed to Polly as she lay in bed and listened to it that first night, that the ticking of the clock was making a prisoner of time. Caging it in.

"And making me a prisoner, too," she thought. And then, "Didn't make prisoners of time of *them*, though. Slipped the net of time, that's what he said. And them dancers — spinning round that pole they were, free as birds!"

And thinking of birds brought her mind full circle again, to Tom, and she wept for a while into her pillow.

With Tom and Alice gone, Polly spent more and more time escaping from Aunt Em's kingdom and into her own. The very next day she went, and when she reached the lake stood and gazed out at it with a kind of desperation. It was busy and alive enough, with its ducks and geese, and here and there broods of tiny bobbing chicks, but Polly vaguely knew that this was not enough. She wanted something more.

"Wonder if it might have a monster, like Loch Ness?" she thought. "*That'd* liven things up!"

But she knew this to be unlikely, and so went wandering further into the woodland, treading paths that were new to her. And as she went the voices came again, and the laughter, and children singing, and she began to run, because it felt as if they — whoever they were — were playing hide and seek. They were tantalising her, daring her to follow. In the end she had to stop for lack of breath. She decided to try something else.

"Come out!" she called loudly. "Come out! I am the

Queen of this kingdom, and I command you!"

After that she heard no more voices. She was left feeling not only alone, but also rather silly. And feeling silly made her mad.

"I'll wake you up," she shouted, and began to stamp furiously on the ground. "I'll wake you up, down there!"

"Am I stamping on their sky?" she wondered. "Am I being thunder?"

She set off. "Stamp stamp wake up! Stamp stamp wake up!" she chanted as she went. "Stamp stamp w —!"

A man and woman were sitting on a bench nearby and watching her with astonishment. She felt her face burn. Then the woman nudged the man and laughed. Polly fled. She ran deep, deeper into the woods, and so it was that she came upon the bluebells. She stopped dead.

They stretched as far as she could see, acres of them it seemed, just on the point of breaking into flower. They lay as a faint blue mist under the trees, marvellously blue, the distilled essence of blueness itself.

"Beautiful!" gasped Polly out loud. "Oh, if only Dad could see them!"

She stared entranced, the voices forgotten. Then she stooped and began to pick.

"Take 'em to Aunt Em," she thought. "Even *she'll* see they're beautiful."

She straightened up and took one last look at the expanse of blue. She vowed to herself to come back every single day as long as they were in flower.

"Might never see so many again," she thought. "Not so long as I live."

Just then a cuckoo called, and to Polly the moment was made perfect.

She wandered dreamily away, taking the path she thought would lead her back to the lake. All at once she turned a corner, and saw to her left a number of flat stone slabs, each fenced in by iron railings.

"Whatever...?" she wondered out loud.

She went over and read the inscription on the first tablet:

*Snuffy, The Pet Dog of
Miss L. Saville Lumley
died December 23rd 1893.*

"They're animal graves!" said Polly. "Well — that is posh!"

She passed on, reading each inscription aloud.

"'Boris. Faithful friends are hard to find.'

Hmmm. *That's* true, right enough. Boris... *That's* a funny name for a dog. Wonder what he was like...?"

Polly Flint stood and wondered and as she did so raised her eyes and saw, watching her from a few feet away, a dog. He was black, except for a white bib and shoes. Polly gaped at the dog and he sat and gazed back — or so far as she could tell. He was so shaggy that his eyes were almost hidden. All the time her mind was racing.

"Could it be ... could it... ? Can't! You can't have ghosts of *dogs*!"

They held their gaze, the pair of them, while the cuckoos called about them.

"Boris!" said Polly softly at last.

He came then. He was at her feet wagging his tail, and she was patting him and saying, "Good boy, good boy!" and there was no possibility of his being a ghost because he was warm and soft and solid, and she felt his breath on her hands. He ran off a little way. Then

62

he stopped and looked back as if expecting her to follow. So she did, and then called again, "Boris!" and again he came to the call, as if knowing the name as his own.

This time she knelt and felt in the fur at his neck for a collar, but her fingers encountered not leather, but a large-linked chain, slightly rusty.

"No name!" she exclaimed, light-headed with relief. "No name and address!"

She hugged him, and scratched under his chin as you would a cat, and he rolled over on his back, all four paws waving in the air, and Polly knew that he must be hers.

She stopped scratching, and he rolled back on to his feet again and sat looking at her, waiting.

"Listen, Boris," she said, and was surprised to find her voice trembling. "I'm going to keep you, I am, no matter what! D'you want to stop with me? Do you?"

His tail moved. He watched her intently.

"You can tell every word I'm saying," she said. "I know you can. But the thing is, you see, I've got this Aunt Em, and I'm stopping with her. Not for ever, but for a bit. And the thing is, I bet you my last currant bun she don't like dogs!"

He looked up at her — expectantly, it seemed.

"Come along with me," she said, getting to her feet again. "And what we'll do, when we get there, you stop outside while I sneak in and get a brush and comb. She might just like *clean* dogs, I suppose!"

Polly sounded more hopeful than she felt. She marched very straight along the path toward the lake, and the dog trotted beside her like a little black shadow.

"Bit of a funny old name, Boris," she said thoughtfully. "Sounds a bit foreign, if you don't mind me saying."

He made no response, one way or the other.

"Could shorten it. I wonder...?" she turned the matter over. "Boz!"

The dog stopped. He looked up.

"Good old boy, Boz!" He wagged his tail. "Come on, Boz!"

She started off again and so did he.

"Isn't it a wonder," said Polly Flint aloud and to nobody in particular, "how the world can change from one minute to the next!"

When they reached Forge Cottage she stopped.

"Stay!" she commanded in a loud whisper. The dog sat. "Good old Boz!" she whispered. "Shan't be long!"

Very gently she turned the knob and pushed open the door. She was greeted by the heavily ticking clock. She listened a moment. All was quiet.

"In the garden, round the back," she decided.

She stole upstairs, took her brush and comb from the dressing table and peered down from the window. There Boz sat exactly as she had left him. She felt like shouting aloud. She crept down again.

"Good boy!" she told him. The tail thumped. "Going to smarten you up a bit. Bit of a scallywag you look."

He stood patiently while she brushed and combed his tousled coat. His look seemed reproachful.

"It's only for Aunt Em," she told him. "Fussy. Much too clean. Eat your dinner off the floor. Now stop there, and I'll go and fetch her."

She picked up the bluebells from the table. Aunt Em was hoeing her weedless garden.

"Wonder is she doesn't dust it," Polly thought. "And vacuum the lawn. And polish the pansies."

She giggled. Aunt Em turned. Polly straightened

her face. This was not a good beginning.

"I've got you these, Aunt Em," she said, holding out the bluebells.

"What? Oh! Bluebells! You've never got them out the park?"

Polly nodded.

"Then you shouldn't. There's notices everywhere telling you not to pick things. Look well if you'd have been caught! Whatever would the neighbours've said!"

"I didn't notice," Polly stammered. "I'm sorry!" This particular bunch of flowers was not going to make anything easier.

"Aunt Em..." Polly said. "I've something to show you."

"Oh yes?"

"Well, not exactly some *thing*."

There was no reply.

"Will you come and look, then?"

"Won't it wait?"

"I'm not sure if it will or not!" said poor Polly. What if he ran off? What if he saw a cat, or a rabbit? "*Please* come!"

Aunt Em stepped back on to the path and sighed.

"It's out at the front," Polly told her.

Aunt Em was extremely startled when confronted with Boz.

"*Whatever*?" she exclaimed.

"He's a stray. I found him in the wood and he's got no collar and no address so I brought him home," Polly gabbled. "He's ever so good and he does everything you tell him, and —"

"Stop!" Aunt Em held up a hand and stared down at Boz with unconcealed distaste.

"*That* ain't a deal of a dog," she observed at last.

"Whatever make is it? Nothing *I've* ever seen before!"

"I don't know," admitted Polly. "But he's got a nice face."

"If you could see it!" said Aunt Em tartly, but not without justification.

"He's ever so friendly," said Polly quickly. "Aren't you, Boz old boy?"

He got up then and advanced, wagging his tail. Aunt Em rapidly dropped back several paces.

"He likes you!" cried Polly.

"*What's* his name? *What* was that you called him?"

"Boz," said Polly. She left out the part about Boris. She had the feeling that ghosts and foreigners would be suspect alike. "It just came into my head. Can I keep him, Aunt Em? Can I, please?"

"You certainly cannot," replied Aunt Em promptly. "I never heard of such a thing!"

"But can't he stop till we've found him a home? He was lost — he's a stray. We can't just turn him back loose in the woods. Besides," she added with cunning, "somebody might report us to the RSPCA."

"I hold no truck with animals in the house," said Aunt Em. "But now you've brought him, you'd better get him off the doorstep. Are his feet clean?"

And so Boz gained a foothold in Aunt Em's kingdom, against all likelihood, because of her fear of what the neighbours might say. And once he had sniffed about him and was satisfied, he settled himself down with his nose between his paws and there was nothing at all in his behaviour for Aunt Em to take exception to.

That night Alice telephoned and Polly told her about the dog, and when Alice asked to speak to Aunt Em, and the upshot of it all was that Boz was to be allowed to stay, for the time being.

"We shall have to advertise, of course," she said. "In the Lost and Found. Only thing is — what to *describe* him as."

That night Boz slept on a blanket by Polly's bed. Aunt Em had objected very strongly to this at first, but when she had run through the list of other possibilities, which were *her* kitchen, *her* sitting and dining room and *her* landing, the thing was inevitable.

"It's unhygienic, of course," she told Polly, when she came up to say goodnight. "It's to be hoped you don't catch anything. Enough trouble in the family, as it is."

When she had gone Polly began to tell Boz in a low whisper about the magic. She told him about the maypole and that secret dawn when the May Dancers had come, about the voices and echoes, the glimpses of figures in the woods.

"And this weekend," she concluded, "we'll go there, we will, and you'll sniff 'em out for me!" She wondered fleetingly whether ghosts — daydreams — Time Gypsies — *had* scents, but thrust the thought away.

"In any case," she thought, "Boz could be a Time *Dog*."

Before settling herself to sleep she took her usual last look at the maypole. She did not really expect to see anything. Light streamed from The Red Lion opposite, and cars came and went, momentarily flooding the green with light. But this had become a ritual, that on waking, and again last thing at night, she held tryst with whatever magic it was that haunted this place.

A solitary figure passed over a lighted patch of the green, seeming gigantic, footlinked with his own shadow. Old Mazy.

"And *he* fits in somewhere," she thought, as she let the curtains fall.

Chapter 4

When she woke next morning Polly looked straight away to see if Boz was still there. He had, after all, appeared under very strange circumstances.

"He is!" Her relief was enormous.

He came over and put his two front paws on the bed, and she told him, "We're going hunting today, you and me!"

She gave his blanket a good shake out of the window, tidied her own bed with extra care, and went down, light-hearted as she had not been for ages. Even the ticking of the grandfather clock seemed less ominous today.

When she had run errands for Aunt Em and fetched dog food from the shop, she and Boz set off for the lake. She went first, as queen, to the wooden landing stage, where she threw crusts for her courtier ducks.

"I know why they've let me keep you," she told Boz. "It's to keep me company. I can read 'em like an open book. And so you are — company, I mean. But of course, a dog ain't a Dad, Boris old lad. Hey — that rhymed! A dog ain't a Dad, Boz old lad! Not a brother or sister, either. Always wanted one. But Mam couldn't, see. One of those things, she says — whatever that means."

She stood up and brushed off the crumbs.

"Ah well! Come on! We're hunting, remember!" Polly deliberately avoided the path that led to the animal graves. She did not exactly believe that Boz would vanish there just as he had appeared, but it seemed wise not to take any risks. She wandered along the path by the lakeside and looked yet again at the island that had a curious, arched tunnel running from one side to the other.

"What's *that* for?" she wondered out loud.

She gazed for a while, and was about to walk on when she turned back with a gasp. There — in the water — a reflection! She stood absolutely still, hardly daring to breathe. She craned forward to see the better, and made out that it was a boy — water rippled, of course, because of the swimming ducks — but a boy, right enough, and doing something with his hands... holding something....

There it was! Very faint and far away, the sound of a fiddle. "Polly put the kettle on, Polly put the kettle on."

Slowly, very slowly, trying not to move her head, but swivelling her eyes as far as she could to her left, she sought the original of the reflection. Nothing! She looked down again at the water. Gone.

At her side sat Boz, patiently waiting. Had he seen, she wondered? Dogs were supposed to have a sixth sense, to see things invisible to human eyes.

"Did *you* see, Boz?" she asked.

He looked up at her, and his tail moved ever so slightly, but Polly could make neither a "yes" nor a "no" of his answer.

She took a final long look into the lake, but the image had gone, and the music faded, and she was left yet again clutching at straws. What was it that Old Mazy had said about the lake...?

"Water always finds its own level..."

What could he *mean*?

She happened to look up at that moment, and caught sight of a stationary figure at the far side of the lake. As she watched, an arm was raised in

70

greeting. It was Old Mazy himself. She waved back, but she did not want his company. The park was big enough to lose fifty people in, let alone one, and she quickened her step and soon took one of the little paths that led away from the lake and into Broad Ride, the wide grassy avenue that in the old days had led to the great Abbey beyond. She crossed that, too, and was soon meandering along a narrow track with trees on either hand, lacing their boughs overhead.

"Won't find me *here*!" she thought.

When she first saw the bluebell haze again through the trees, she was again flooded by an astonishing sense of sheer blueness. The very air above them was so thickly blue that she almost felt that she could touch it.

"Though I expect it'd be like a rainbow," she thought. "When you get up to it — gone!"

And like the Time Gypsies, too, for that matter. Elusively there at a distance, but always ahead no matter how hard you ran.

Polly stopped. Boz looked up enquiringly.

"I've tried chasing," she said. "But I've never tried *calling*. I reckon the time has come to call."

She wheeled about, scanning for hints, whispers, signs.

"Hallo!" she called. And then again, "Hallo! I'm Polly Flint, and I want to be your friend!"

She listened, and heard only the usual small noises of a wood.

"And also," she called, "I am Queen, and this is my kingdom!"

Boz began to veer off to the right of the path, his nose close to the ground.

"Tracking!" she thought. "He's got a scent!"

71

She followed him then as fast as she could, and saw that he had stopped among the bluebells. His plumy tail was waving above them. She wove her way through to him, and whatever it was she had expected to see it was not what she saw now. It lay wrapped in a bundle of bluish cloth and its eyes were wide open and tiny fists opening and closing as if plucking at something invisible in the air.

"A baby!" gasped Polly. Then, "Whose? Whatever...?"

It began to make little gurgling noises. Boz had finished his exploratory sniffing, and now sat squared and fixed by the baby's head, as if a self-appointed guardian. His chain, hanging medallion-like down his front, added to the impression that his position was official.

Polly dropped to her knees. She did not quite know what to say to a baby — particularly a baby that might be at least five hundred years old. There was no way of telling, she thought. Bundled up babies must have all looked more or less the same since the world began.

"Been left," she said out loud. "Like Moses in the bulrushes."

The baby gazed up at her. Polly liked its wide bright eyes, its friendliness. Hesitantly she held out her hand and it was held, quite tightly, by the tiny grubby fingers. A marvellous thought came to her.

"First Boz," she said, "and now you. Perhaps — perhaps *you're* meant for me, as well!"

Her mind reeled and raced at the thought. She had just got to the point where she tried to think how she would introduce the baby to Aunt Em, when she heard a call behind her. To her amazement, Boz stiffened, stood for a moment with his head cocked, then raced away. She leapt to her feet, and heard a second call.

"Baggins! Baggins!"

And now at last Polly Flint saw them plain. After all the shadows, echoes and reflections, after all the vain pursuits, there, at last, they were. She could not see their faces yet, because they were bending over Boz, patting and praising him, and seeing this she was torn between exultation and annoyance.

"Just as if they owned him!" she thought.

"Boz!" she called. "Come on — come on, boy!"

To her delight he came, and so did the boy, lit in flashes as the sunlight struck him. A man followed more slowly behind him. They stopped a few yards away. Boz was back at his post by the baby again.

"It's no use your doing that now, you heathen!" The boy was wagging a finger at him. "Set to *guard* him, you were. Where've you been?"

"He's been with me," said Polly boldly. "I'm Polly Flint and he's *my* dog."

The pair of them looked at her now, up and down.

"Stuff," the boy said. "He's ours. Ain't you, Baggins?"

"Boz — come on Boz, good boy!"

He rose and trotted to her outstretched hand.

"See?" she cried triumphantly.

"See nothing!" the boy said. "Baggins — here, come on!"

He trotted towards the outstretched hand.

"See?" he mocked. Polly's mind was racing. *Was* he their dog? He was, after all, a stray — though whether in space or time she could not know.

"All right," she said, "if he's yours, how long've you had him? And where did you get him?"

"We found him," the boy said. "Finder's keepers.

73

And never mind how long. We don't care about how long — time's nothing."

Polly looked at him, taking in the ragged shirt and breeches that looked several sizes too big for him. In one hand he held a fiddle and a bow. His feet were bare.

"Time mightn't mean anything to *you*," she said deliberately. "Because you're Time Gypsies."

There was no reply. They gazed at her, hard and long. The boy's expression changed to one of suspicion — even fear.

"She's on to us," he said at last.

"She sees us," said the man, "*and* hears us."

"Just our luck! *Two* of 'em now, stalking and hunting!"

"She's been on to us from the start. She was there at the May Dancing."

"*And* The Catcher!"

Polly was not pleased to be discussed as if she were not there.

"I am *here*, you know," she said. "I can see you and I can hear you."

"That's just it," said the boy glumly. He looked hard at Polly.

"You called us Time Gypsies," he said. "How did you know?"

"Someone told me."

The pair exchanged glances.

"The Catcher!" said the man. "There's only him could've told her."

"P'raps she's in with him!" The boy looked swiftly about him. "Could've sent her to trap us!"

They were frightened now, both man and boy, and Polly found it unbearable to think that it was because of her.

"Don't be frightened!" she cried. "Please! I'm not in with anybody, honest I'm not. I want to be friends."

They stood there uncertainly, all three of them, and Polly wondered desperately what she might do to make them believe her. Then, beyond them, she saw figures approaching.

"Look out!" she cried. "Hide! Somebody's coming!"

They did not even turn their heads.

"There's a whole family!" she cried.

"Better pick *him* up, I s'pose," said the boy, jerking his head towards the baby. "Don't want him trod on."

He bent and picked up the grubby bundle.

"I warned you," Polly said.

"Now listen here," the boy said, "*we* don't need to hide. We see them, but they don't see us."

"There's only you *can*," said the man, "so far as we know. You and The Catcher, maybe."

"Of course!" This she had quite forgotten. Now that she at last could see them, the notion that the Time Gypsies were invisible seemed absurd — impossible, almost.

The figures were now scattered and picking bluebells, except for one, a boy, who was still advancing.

"It's Polly Flint!" She saw that it was Davey Cole.

"Who was you talking to, just now?"

"I was talking to Boz," Polly said.

"That your dog?"

"Yes, it is, as a matter of fact."

"Can it see where it's going?" He sniggered.

"As a matter of fact he can. As a matter of fact, he can see better than *you* can."

"*Very* likely," said Davey, "through all that fur!"

"*And* hear better," said Polly. "Hear that baby crying, can you?"

75

"What baby?" He looked about him. "There ain't one."

Polly smiled sweetly.

"Funny. I could swear I hear one crying."

"You're barmy. Daft."

"One of us is," said Polly. "Come on, Boz!"

She started to walk away, but kept a sidelong eye on the Time Gypsies as she went. She supposed they could slip out of sight as suddenly as they had appeared — for all she knew they would vanish — melt into thin air before her very eyes.

They were following her. As soon as she was out of earshot of Davey Cole she stopped, and waited for them.

"What did you say your name was?" the boy asked.

"Polly Flint. What's yours?"

"Don't tell!" said the boy quickly.

"Why not?" Polly was indignant. "I told mine."

"It'll give her power over us," he told the man.

"She already has," he returned. "She sees and hears us."

"I don't *want* power over you!" Polly was quite desperate. "I want us to be friends."

"We'll tell," the man said. "Not a deal more harm to be done, now. I'm Gil."

She looked enquiringly at the boy.

"Sam," he muttered at last, reluctantly.

"And what about the baby?" Polly asked.

"Ain't got a name, not yet," Gil said. "Hasn't been named yet, by parson. Babby Porter, that's what he gets called."

"And he's a great fat nuisance," Sam said. "One of these days he'll get trod on. But you can't lug *that* lump round all day."

"Gil! Gil! Sam! Sam!" A thin cracked voice floated

76

through the trees.

"It's Granny Porter," said Gil. He raised his voice. "Here!"

The oddest figure was approaching. At first Polly could not make it out, and even when she did, it seemed more like a bush or a shrub that had suddenly sprouted feet, than like a human being. The shape advanced with a curious hobbling gait, and seemed to be moving both sideways and forwards at once. As it approached, a low mutter was to be heard.

"In and out up and down day to night dawn to dusk!"

"She ain't going to be none too pleased about *her*!" said Sam, meaning Polly.

The figure was dressed in stitched tatters of a thousand mucky rags, that looked like the plumage of a particularly frowsty large bird. The face was at first invisible on account of a large and bedraggled bonnet.

"Up and down in and out," came the mutter again.

"Here we are, then, Granny!" exclaimed Gil, with an attempt at cheerfulness.

"Here?" snapped the bonnet. "Where's here? Up down in and out, here there and everywhere!"

"Now then, Granny," said Gil soothingly. "World's still spinning!"

"World? World? *Me* that's spinning. My poor old head, round and round in and out up and down here and —"

"Look you what's here, Granny," interrupted Gil to prevent a further flow.

The bonnet lifted. Polly saw the oldest, most crisscrossed and wrinkled face she had ever seen.

"She must be a *hundred*!" she thought. "At least!"

And yet the eyes were not old. The eyes were amazingly bright and quick and birdlike. They looked at Polly long and hard.

"Who's that?" she snapped. "That ain't one of ours!"

"No, Granny," agreed Gil.

"Oooh! I knew there'd be ill luck!" she wailed. "We're not spotted! Never say we're spotted!"

She glared at Polly with such intensity that she fell back a couple of paces.

"Give that Babby Porter here to me!" she said, snatching the baby from Sam. "Wicked it is, a little babby being risked up here. How do we know there's not wolves?"

"Oh, there aren't any wolves," said Polly, pleased to have something to add to the conversation. "You don't get wolves, not in England."

Silence. The old lady fixed Polly with yet another glowering look.

"So she *does* see us, does she?" she said slowly and terribly. "And hears us. *She's* our ill luck!"

"Now go easy, Granny," said Gil. "She's nobbut a little lass."

"And I'm not bad luck!" said Polly passionately. "I'm not, I'm *not*."

"Then why does she see us?" demanded Granny Porter. "And hear us?"

"I do see things," Polly told her. She added, proudly, "One day, I saw an angel."

They stared at her, all three.

"You saw *what*?" hissed the old woman.

"An *angel*?" repeated Gil incredulously.

Polly nodded.

"Not that they believed me," she said, "any more than they would if I told 'em about *you*!"

"And why not, *pray*?" The raggy plumage was all a-twitch and a-quiver. "We're *here*, ain't we? Which is more than angels is."

"All I mean is," said poor Polly, "that if I do see you, and nobody else does, they'll think you aren't real."

Granny Porter advanced.

"Here — you take this!" She thrust the baby at Gil. "We — ain't — *what*?"

"Oh — I don't know!" wailed Polly. "I'm all mixed up. But there's a real world over there —" she waved an arm vaguely about her — "a world with cars and buses and TV and my Aunt Em and — and — fish fingers! And none of *you* —"

She faltered.

"Go on," said the old lady dangerously. "None of us — what?"

"Oh, it's not fair!" Polly burst out. "You think it's you that's real and me that's not, just because there's more of you. You're three to one!" She looked at the baby. "Four to one!"

"Four to two," corrected Sam. "You've got our Baggins."

"She's what?" Granny Porter sounded dangerous again.

"Got Baggins, Granny. Must've fed him."

There was a long pause. Granny Porter shook her head and hissed softly between her teeth.

"I don't understand," said Polly, "I honestly don't. Of course I fed him. What difference does that make?" Another silence. Polly was aware of secret looks exchanged, a mystery.

"Never mind," said Gil at last. "It does."

"She gives me the creeps," said Sam. "Ain't used to being seen."

"It's you that ought to give *me* the creeps!" said

79

Polly indignantly. "At least I'm here — properly here, I mean!"

She was back on the old dangerous ground. Granny Porter held up a hand and wagged a finger.

"Never you cross me, girl," she said, and there was a hint of menace in her looks, so that Polly suddenly shivered. "You beware of me — just as I must beware of you!"

Polly shook her head dumbly.

"You have powers," Granny Porter went on, "just as I have powers."

"Come on," said Sam then, tugging at Gil's sleeve. His face was pinched and scared. "Let's go! She's got our Baggins — how do we know she won't get us?"

"Best to go, yes," Gil agreed. "Let things be now, Granny. There's no harm done."

"No harm done but harm to come," the soft voice crooned. Then she turned, and Polly saw only the bonnet and the raggedy figure was shuffling off without another word to say.

"Farewell," said Gil, and turned to follow.

"And you look after our Baggins!" Sam said, and darted after them.

Polly watched them go, that strange trio under the slanting shafts of sunlight.

"*Where* will they go?" she wondered. "And what will they do?"

"Will you come again?" she called after them. All she had in reply was a slow raising of an arm from Gil, his back still turned.

"Could mean *owt*, that could," she said. She looked down at Boz who sat watching them too. "Least you didn't follow them. Mine, you are. Have you been under earth?" He looked up at her. "Pity dogs can't talk. Pity..."

She sighed. They were out of sight now.

"Come on!" said Polly. "We'll follow 'em!"

But the Time Gypsies had gone, there was neither sight nor sound of them.

"Could they have gone invisible again?" she wondered. "Or back under earth. And if they do go under earth — how do they get down there? Secret tunnel... or lift, like at pit..." She laughed then. "And that's a funny thing... If there is a village down there, with people living in houses, and that, why don't the coal miners see them..?"

She shook her head. It was all beyond her. Polly Flint wandered on through her kingdom, marvelling at the thought that under her very feet, beneath the bracken, the moss and the bluebells, was another world and, most amazing, another time.

"It's a puzzle!" she said out loud.

She was now by the pool she named the Silver Pool because of the birches reflected in its waters.

"It ain't much fun being a queen if there's nobody to command," she told Boz. "Excepting you, of course. I wish — oh *how* I wish them Time Gypsies had stopped!"

And then the wood was suddenly peopled. It was the strangest thing. One minute she was standing there alone gazing at the pool and its quiet reflections, and the next there was thin, echoing laughter, voices, music — and there, flitting from tree to tree, children, fast and slippery as quicksilver and quite certainly and beyond question brought there by magic.

Then the small figure of a boy advanced to the very edge of the pool, and he raised a fiddle and started to play. His eyes met Polly's, and she saw that it was her boy — Sam

81

"Not gone!" she breathed.

The tune he played floated over to where she stood.

Polly put the kettle on
Polly put the kettle on,
Polly put the kettle on
We'll all have tea!

"For me!" she thought. "He's playing it for me!" and stood straight and proud as any queen.

"All those children," she thought, "a *maypoleful* of children, and all singing for me!"

The song came to an end and the children ran forward and bowed and Polly clapped her hands.

"Hurray!" she cried.

The fiddle struck up again, and this time it was "Ring a Ring o' Roses". The children ran together to join hands but all at once a cry went up from one of them,

"The Catcher! The Catcher!"

They screamed and scattered, crying "The Catcher! The Catcher!" as they fled. The tune came to an abrupt end. Bewildered and scared, Polly scanned about her and saw, through the trees, that same striding figure she had glimpsed before in the woods. He went with slow huge strides as he had gone before, and in one hand brandished a long stick curved like a shepherd's crook, and in the other a giant net.

"The Catcher!" shrieked Polly, and began to run as fast as she could, because although the pool lay between her and that awful shape it seemed to her that he might come striding on right over the water, and she herself become enmeshed in that terrible net.

She ran pell mell and not caring where she went, and stopped only when she felt a sharp stitch in her side. Under a low, widely branched tree she crouched, and tried to listen, above her own heavy breathing, for sounds of pursuit. Limply she dropped to the ground.

"Can't run any more!" she gasped, and took hold of Boz's chain to stop him running out and betraying her hiding place.

"Oh dear! I don't know *when* I'll dare to come out from here!" she told him. "We'll have to stop here *ages*. And then I'll be late for dinner, and Aunt Em'll be mad at me!"

She was, too. When she finally emerged she ran all the way back, because she did not know where that figure might be striding now, or whether at any moment a giant net might drop from nowhere over her head.

For once, Forge Cottage almost seemed like home.

"Lucky it's nothing that'd spoil," said Aunt Em, ladling stew on to the plates. "Didn't you *know* what time it was?"

"Haven't got a watch," gasped Polly, still trying to get her breath.

"Then you should have!" she retorted, and then, as an afterthought, "Though even if you had, you'd lose it, I suppose."

Polly thought for a little.

"Aunt Em," she said, "do you believe in time?"

"Do I...? Now what kind of a ridiculous question is that? Of course I believe in time."

"Why?" asked Polly.

"Because — because time's time, that's why!" replied Aunt Em lamely.

"Ah, but what if it *wasn't*?" said Polly. "Suppose it wasn't?"

"I shall suppose no such silly thing!" snapped Aunt Em.

"I don't know where you get your ideas from, I really don't."

Polly was making a pattern in her stew with her fork.

"Polly — *don't*!"

"Polly Don't, again," thought Polly. "*Should* be my name, and that's a fact."

She munched a little and went on thinking.

"Aunt Em," she said, "you know my park..."

"Do I know what? It's Rufford you mean, I suppose."

"Well — have you ever heard... any stories about it?"

"Stories? What kind of stories?"

"I don't exactly know," said Polly. She thought, "I can't tell her. Mustn't. Wouldn't believe me in any case." Out loud she said, "*Legend* kind of stories."

"I've heard nothing," said Aunt Em. "There's nothing *to* hear."

"Oh, but there is," thought Polly Flint. "I could tell you a story, a *true* story, that'd make you *goggle*!"

"I don't know what you find to do there all day," Aunt Em told her. "I hope you don't go getting near that lake."

"Not near enough to fall in," said Polly. "And even if I did, I should soon swim out again. This is very nice stew, Aunt Em."

"Oh!" she said. She was almost, but not quite, sidetracked. "The day you drop in that lake," she observed, "will be the last day you ever go near it."

"Yes, Aunt Em," said Polly meekly.

There was a silence — or at any rate as near a silence as was possible in that particular house.

84

"That grandfather clock's got a very loud tick," said Polly.

"It was my mother's," said Aunt Em, as if that accounted for the matter. "And her mother's, before that. It's never lost a single second."

Polly looked at her aunt and gave a little sigh.

"I don't expect it *dare*," she thought. "Not in *this* house!"

After dinner she went up to her room to write a letter to Tom. She spent a long time sucking her pencil before she decided.

"Shall I, or shan't I...?" she wondered. She pictured Tom in his high hospital bed, staring at the ceiling and seeing his own private skyful of birds.

"All day long, just lying there..." she thought. "I *shall* tell him!"

And so she began, "Dear Dad, I hope you are well and feeling better, and here is what has been happening to me. You know that lake I told you about, with all the birds..."

And she went on and described it all, exactly as it had happened, she told of the echoing laughter and silvery voices, and then of her meeting with the Time Gypsies, and she named them, Gil, Sam, and Granny Porter.

"And then there's Babby Porter," she added, "and they *only* call him Babby Porter, can you believe!"

Then she wrote of the scene by the Silver Pool, and how The Catcher came striding by with net and crook; her own heart thudded as she remembered it. When she read it over, she decided that Alice might be frightened by it, so she added, "But you mustn't worry, because I have Boz and I expect he would guard me."

She looked down at Boz where he lay slumped,

nose between paws, and wondered about this.

"He certainly don't *look* like a guarding kind of a dog," she thought. "And come to think, he didn't make much of a job of guarding Babby Porter!"

She turned back to the letter, and added, "I miss you, Mam and Dad, I really do."

She sucked again on her pencil and tried to think up a rhyme for Tom.

"And now I'm ending with a rhyme, to say I don't believe in time!"

She put the letter in its envelope.

"Don't, either!" she thought, and went downstairs to ask for a stamp. "You sent my love, I hope," said Aunt Em as she fished in her purse.

"Oh yes," said Polly. But it was not true.

"Hadn't thought of love, in connection with her," she thought.

"You weren't thinking of going down Rufford again this afternoon, I hope?" said Aunt Em.

"Oh yes!" said Polly, dismayed.

"Then you'll need to think again," said Aunt Em. "You can come along of me, collecting."

"Collecting?" echoed Polly.

"For the jumble," Aunt Em nodded. "W.I. jumble, today week. We'll go knocking round and see what there is. I shall need you to help carry."

"Yes Aunt Em," said Polly. She did not really mind, when she thought about it. "Might not have *dared* to go back there," she thought. "Not with The Catcher about."

Besides, she liked jumble. She had often helped Alice collect it, and liked to rummage through it, seeing things that other people threw away, and sometimes fishing bits and pieces out for herself, before other people got the chance.

"Just post this letter, then," she said.

She went out and over the green and looked up, as usual, at the maypole, acknowledging its magic. There sat Old Mazy on his usual bench, his head tipped back and eyes seeming to be closed. But as she drew near he suddenly opened his eyes wide and his head came up.

"Good day, Polly Flint," he said.

"Good afternoon," replied Polly politely, and was going to walk straight on past him, when she felt something catch at her ankle, and stumbled and fell.

"Oh!" she gasped. "Whatever?"

And she saw that he had used the crook of his long stick to trip her, and she stared up into his dark face with terror.

"The Catcher," she thought. "Oh, my moon and stars — he must be The Catcher!"

Chapter 5

"Don't you do that!" gasped Polly, getting up and looking around for her dropped letter.

"Just a little game I play," he said. "No need to be afeared of Old Mazy. Harmless enough."

She stared at him. Could it be he she had seen striding like a giant through the woods?

"Reflections were there today?" he asked her. "Voices?"

"No!' said Polly loudly, rubbing at her knees. "No, there weren't!"

"My old eyes aren't so good, you see," he went on. "These days, I only seem to be able to see things that are really there. Do you take my meaning, Polly Flint?"

"No!" she stammered, and backed away a little, wary of the curved stick. "No, I don't!"

"Ah, but I think you do," he said softly. "Heard the bells, didn't you? Saw the children in the wood?"

"I must've been mistaken!" she cried. "I — I'm always imagining things. You ask my Mam!"

"Oh, I shan't do that," he said. "No need at all of that. I shall just do as I always have. Watch — and wait."

"I've to go now." Polly backed right off. "Got a letter to post!" and she ran all the way there and back again. She took care to take the other side of the green, but gave a sideway look as she went by, and saw the bench empty.

"Gone!" she thought. "Gone down to Rufford? Oh, and I can't even warn 'em! Oh — blow the jumble!"

Back at Forge Cottage she called "Aunt Em!" and

receiving no reply went out to the back and found her struggling to pull something out of the shed.

"There!" she gasped, with a final yank.

"Whatever?" Polly gaped. It was a pram, a big pram with enormous wheels, and covered with dust and cobwebs which Aunt Em was already busily flicking away.

"Is that for the jumble?" she asked.

"For collecting," said Aunt Em. "Comes in very handy for collecting."

"But where's it from?" asked Polly. "It does look old!"

"It was mine," said Aunt Em, "when I was a baby. And your mam's. Used to push her in it, I did."

"But whatever did you keep it for?" cried Polly. "That was years and years ago!"

"Waste not, want not!" said Aunt Em, blushing red and looking awkward all the same.

"She could never've thought she'd get a baby to put in it!" thought Polly. "That'd be the day — her to have a baby!"

And she giggled at the thought, and Aunt Em heard the giggle, and said "Look sharp, now — out the way!"

They set off round the village and within an hour the pram was filled to overflowing. Polly watched her aunt pushing the enormous pram before her, and more than once thought, "She looks as pleased as punch with herself! You'd almost think there *was* a baby in there!" and allowed herself another giggle at the thought.

"Now, then," said Aunt Em, pushing the laden pram up the step. "That'll do for now. We'll sort it all out later. But what I'll do, Polly, as you've been such a good help, I'll come a little walk along with you, down Rufford."

"Oh!" Polly's hand flew to her mouth to stifle her gasp of dismay. "What if they're there? What if she *sees* them?"

"Well, don't that please you, miss?" demanded Aunt Em, huffy at Polly's want of proper gratitude.

"Oh — yes, yes," lied Polly. "That'll be smashing, Aunt Em."

"We shan't take that dog," said Aunt Em, eyeing the hopeful Boz. "I can be doing without him dancing round my feet."

"Oh, he's ever so good," Polly assured her. "He don't do that. And I'm going to train him to do ever so many other things!"

Aunt Em contented herself with a snort. Boz — or Baggins — stayed behind.

It was strange to Polly to enter Rufford for the first time not alone.

"It's my kingdom," she thought, "and now she's setting foot in it."

But because it *was* her kingdom, Polly soon began to find herself enjoying pointing out this and that to her companion.

"That's the Silver Pool," she told her, as they approached it. "See? Because of them birches."

"Very nice," said Aunt Em.

"And look — see that? A tunnel, going right through from one side of the island to the other. Ain't decided what that's for, yet. So I call it the Secret Tunnel."

"Very nice," said Aunt Em.

"And here's the bluebells!" Polly cried at last. "That I told you about. I brought you some, remember. Look at 'em — miles of 'em."

"Oh, very nice," said Aunt Em. Even she could not

remain unmoved by that glorious blueness. She sighed. "Fair *handsome*," she said. "You've got to admit."

They walked on.

"And now, I shall show *you* something," said Aunt Em.

"What?" cried Polly jealously. This was her kingdom, and she could not bear to think that Aunt Em might know it better than she herself.

"You know who lived there," said Aunt Em, waving towards the Abbey in the distance. "A lot of monks, in the olden times. Though I daresay I'm wrong to say as much to you, if you're to start seeing monks all over everywhere!"

"Oh, I shan't do that," promised Polly. "I've never seen a monk in my life."

"Well, then," said Aunt Em, "You just look at that!"

She pointed. Polly turned and gasped.

"A prison!"

"Prison?" said Aunt Em. "No such thing. You do get carried away, Polly, you really do. It's the Icehouse."

They approached along a dank and shady path. Polly sniffed, and the air seemed already to have an icy tang.

"Still think it looks like a prison," she said.

Cautiously she went up to the massive iron grille and smelled age and cold and darkness. She could not make out the bottom of what seemed an enormous dungeon hollowed beneath the ground. She tested for echoes, and heard her voice flying about her.

"Where the monks used to keep their ice," she heard Aunt Em say from behind her.

"Keep ice? What, all year round? In here?"

"What they say. All I know is, that in the winter they'd dig great blocks of ice, and keep it down there."

"Crikey!" Polly was impressed. "A sort of old-fashioned fridge!"

"Don't believe in fridges, myself," said Aunt Em. "Larder's cool enough for milk and meat, and such. And no-one's ever died for the lack of an ice-cream, so far as I know."

"Hoo! Hoo!" Polly called the echoes out again from the stone.

She shivered and stepped back.

"Don't like it," she said. "Spooky."

"No-one's asking you to like it." Aunt Em was huffy again. "Just trying to teach you summat, that's all."

They walked back along the mossed path and over the Broad Rise with its view of the Abbey over the high yew hedge.

"Long way to carry ice," Polly thought. "Or might there be a tunnel? An underground tunnel...?"

She heard the crying of a baby then, and stiffened. She looked rapidly about her.

"Can't see one," she thought. "Gosh — let them not be there now, let 'em not! If they are — and she sees 'em — they'll think I gave 'em away!"

On the other hand, she reflected, Aunt Em was so very firmly planted in this world, that it was very unlikely that she should even suspect the existence of another.

They were walking back along the edge of the lake now, and still there was no sign of Babby Porter, though Polly could still hear the sound of a baby crying faintly from somewhere among the trees.

"I'll have to sit down now," she heard Aunt Em say.

"Give my legs a rest a minute."

She made towards a wooden seat nearby. Polly looked up and let out a gasp of horror.

There, sitting on the far end of the bench, hunched in her bedraggled plumage with her arms wrapped around herself in an attitude of extreme sulk — was Granny Porter.

Polly's mind whirled. What if Aunt Em saw her — and worse, got into conversation with her? Or — worst — what if Aunt Em didn't see her — and *sat* on her!

Polly closed her eyes in anguish at the thought of Aunt Em descending on to that raggedy lap. Slowly she let out her breath and opened them again.

The two ladies were now sitting one on either end of the bench, both staring out at the lake and both apparently oblivious of the other's presence.

"She can't have seen her, surely!" thought Polly. "She'd never've sat next to her — her being so clean, and all!"

For whatever Granny Porter was or was not, she was undeniably grubby. She was, in fact, what even Alice herself, who was clean without being overly so, would describe as downright mucky.

Both ladies were facing towards the lake but in quite a different manner. Aunt Em was watching the broods of tiny ducklings. Granny Porter was wearing a stare that indicated that she was *seeing* nothing at all, but sunk in terrible and gloomy thought.

"Look, Aunt Em!" Polly almost shrieked. "Look at *them*!" She pointed in the direction away from Granny Porter. "Look at them little ducks over there! Ain't they sweet? And see *there* — other side of that island! Look at —"

"I'm quite capable of looking for myself, thank you,

Polly," said Aunt Em. "Do stop *dancing*, child! Sit down here alonger me, and shush up a minute."

Polly eyed with consternation the narrow space between her aunt and the hunched figure beside her. Just then, Granny Porter did at last turn her face, to give Polly a look of pure malevolence.

"You sit there," the look seemed to say, "and *then* see what happens!"

And then, right behind the frayed bonnet, two faces peered from the thicket. Sam and Gil. They were making furious gestures at her, and pointing to the motionless back of Granny Porter.

"Trying to tell me to get her to come?" Polly wondered. "Daren't speak, I don't suppose, with Aunt Em being there. But I can't speak to her, either." So she too started to make grimaces at Granny Porter and stabbed her finger urgently in the direction of the thicket.

"Do stop *fidgeting*!" said Aunt Em, without moving her gaze from the lake. Granny Porter watched Polly narrowly. Then, very slowly she turned her head. Gil and Sam made vigorous beckoning signs. She turned back towards the lake.

Then, with deliberate slowness, she rose and hobbled off to join them, turning to give Polly one last ill-tempered look before disappearing into the shrubbery.

"Oh!" gasped Polly. "I think I *will* sit down — my legs feel all wobbly!"

Aunt Em and she eventually wandered back home to tea and hot crumpets, and spent an evening that was almost companionable, sorting out the pram full of jumble.

Next day was Sunday. Polly itched to be down in Rufford, but knew that she would have to wait until after dinner.

"Can I just teach Boz some tricks before we go to church?" she begged.

"You can if you don't get yourself dirty," said Aunt Em, "and don't annoy the neighbours. Not that I've any belief that *that* animal'll ever do a trick."

"He will then!" Polly was indignant on Boz's behalf. "You watch this. Ought to have a biscuit, really, but I'll bet he'll do it without!"

She faced him.

"Boz, sit!" He sat. "Now, sit up!"

Boz sat up, wavering precariously on his hind quarters.

"There!" she cried triumphantly.

"It's to be hoped you'll not waste any more biscuits on that!" said Aunt Em, and marched back into the kitchen to attend to her roast.

"You're a clever boy," Polly whispered, "Boz — or Baggins — whichever!"

She picked up a ball and went out on to the quiet Sunday morning green.

"We're going to do Fetch," she told him.

She had thrown the ball for him only a few times when she saw Davey Cole approaching, a canvas bag slung over his shoulder, delivering newspapers.

"Here's the hag's." He passed the paper to her. "Why don't you get that lump of fur to take it?"

"I haven't trained him to, not yet," said Polly with dignity. "But I shall."

"Try it," he said. "He might have already been taught it, before you found him."

"All right."

To her delight, and also to her amazement, Boz-Baggins took the newspaper in his mouth and trotted to the open front door.

"There you are! I bet he could do any trick there is, if I taught him."

"Bet he couldn't!"

"What kind of trick, anyway?" Polly felt inclined to take up the challenge, if it was feasible.

"This!" He pushed his face close to hers and crossed his eyes horribly. Then he ran off over the green.

"Easy!" he yelled as he went. "Easy as winking!"

She pulled a face at his retreating back. She saw him again later, as she reached the church porch with Aunt Em. She knew there was no hope of escaping again, to listen for the Grimstone bells, but she glimpsed him, evidently lurking in wait at the far end of the church. She gave him a quelling and pious look as she entered, straight-backed, by her aunt's side. She had, in any case, the moment the Wellow bells started to ring, hastily and secretly put her ear to the ground in the garden, and *thought* she had heard the answering peals below. She did not, in fact, need to hear them now. She knew for certain that there was a village there below, and that it had, indeed, slipped the net of time.

After dinner Polly set off for Rufford with Boz. As she crossed the ford she looked upstream toward the mill race, and saw, ankle deep in the water, a small boy and girl, one with a jam jar, the other with a net.

"Could it be....?" she wondered.

They stood dappled by the sunlight that filtered through the overhanging trees. The girl certainly had an old-fashioned look in her grey dress with a white smock over, and the boy's knee-length trousers, tied round the waist with twine, were baggy, as if several sizes too big for him. As she watched and wondered, they looked up and saw her. They paused for a moment, then turned and scampered off in a shower of spray.

"Must've been," she thought. "Why else would they run off?"

And as she turned into Rufford she wondered again where was the entry to that secret village? A tunnel seemed most likely, one that looked, perhaps, like any ordinary hole in the ground.

"I wonder if *you* know." She eyed Boz. "If you really were Baggins, you might've been down there. Boz — find a hole — find!"

He tore off. Polly had to run fast to catch up with him, and when she did so she saw that he had run to the foot of an old tree stump, and his plumed tail was waving furiously.

"It's a kind of burrow!" Polly exclaimed with delight.

"Dig, Boz, dig!"

Snorting, he disappeared half way into the opening, and threw back earth with his front paws. Back he came again — but not before Polly had glimpsed daylight through the other side of the stump.

"Here — let me look!"

Boz backed out and Polly stooped and peered. She was right. The tunnel went straight from one side to the other of the stump.

"Never mind," she said. "See if you can find another. Hole, Boz, hole!"

He *did* find another — and another, and another. It was clearly a favourite pursuit of his.

Polly decided to abandon the search for a secret tunnel.

"Though it's still a mystery!" she said out loud. "Must be *somewhere* they come and go."

By now she was on the lake path, and looking up

saw what she had never seen there before — a boat.

"Didn't think boats were allowed," she told Boz, who was drinking greedily at the water's edge. "Just for ducks, and such, I thought this lake was."

It was a small wooden rowing boat, unpainted and shabby. And seated in it were two small figures, and suddenly Polly was alert and straining to see them better. They looked like the children she had seen earlier fishing in the ford stream. They were rowing, it seemed, towards the largest of the islands. Polly kept pace with them along the bank, and came to the point where she could see right through the curious arched tunnel that ran from one side to the other.

"That's that tunnel I've wondered about," said Polly to Boz. "*Now* what'll they do?"

The little boat turned.

"Going into it!" She watched. Now the boat was in the gloom of the arch, the figures of the children barely more than outlines against the light beyond. And then — gone! One minute they were there — the next, gone!

Polly blinked hard and rubbed her eyes.

"Gone? Can't've gone! But where —? Quick, Boz, round to the other side!"

She ran as fast as she could along the bank, over the little wooden bridge, past the smallest island and right to the spot where she could see light through the tunnel, see straight through.

She stood breathless and scanned incredulously the whole wide, bare expanse of lake.

"Vanished — into thin air!" she exclaimed. And then, very slowly, "Or — out of time!"

The answer seemed so simple. What was it that Old Mazy had said, more than once?

"Water always finds its own level."

The boat and the children had effortlessly slipped into another time and another place. She stood and she stared and she shivered with a long, cold thrill of excitement that was half fearful.

"You'd best just go round back where you were, Polly," she told herself. "Just to make absolutely *positive* sure."

But she was already sure in her bones, even as she retraced her steps, and not in the least surprised to find the water beyond the island innocent of anything, more than a brood of ducks. They swam slowly and calmly, each leaving a clear and separate V in its wake.

"And now — where are *my* Gypsies?" wondered Polly Flint. "Anywhere, they could be. Like finding a needle in a haystack, or a pin in a pint of peas."

It was, in fact, to prove nothing like so difficult, because it happened that the Time Gypsies were looking for *her*, and at that very moment were no more than a few yards away.

"Aooch!" she squealed, as something touched her arm — a little dirty hand in a raggedy sleeve.

"*Hist!*" Granny Porter tugged hard on Polly's arm. "Here! Come you here!" And then the ragged creature got behind and pushed her, with little rude shoves.

Polly allowed herself to be nudged and pulled into a little thicket. There she saw Sam and Gil sitting, with Babby Porter lying on, the ground between them. They looked unsmilingly up at her.

"You bad bad gel, you bad bad gel!" Granma Porter gave Polly a series of little sharp prods and slaps — she was fairly dancing with fury.

Polly shrank back out of her reach.

"Why? Why? What've I done?"

"What've you done? What've you done — *you* know what you've done. You bad bad gel, you bad bad gel!" It was as if she would have gone on for ever, pinching and slapping, had not Gil said: "Leave her *be*, Granny!"

"Yes, *leave* her, Granny Porter, do!" cried Sam. "If she's more power than you — *then* where'll we all be?" The old woman gave Polly a final shove and stood back, breathless. She shook her fist.

"All night!" she shrieked. "All night! Dew in my boots, dew in my shawl — aches pains and horrible screws in every joint — toes ankles knees elbows —"

"What do you *mean*?" interrupted Polly desperately.

"Now don't you go playing Pretty Polly with me," she retorted. "*You* know what you've done — if you didn't, you couldn't have done it!"

Polly was still trying to work out the meaning of this enigmatic utterance when Gil said, "We don't *know* she did it, Now hold off her, do, will you? My head's fair splitting."

Polly looked at him. He did indeed look pale. He had a tired, unshaven look such as she had sometimes seen Tom wear when he came for breakfast after the night shift.

Grandma Porter gave a final flap of her shrubbery sleeve in the direction of Polly, and turned her back. Polly, left facing the bonnet, was at a loss how to address it.

"We've been here all night," said Sam. "All night — d'you know that?"

"But why? And what's that to do with me?"

"It's to do with summat," said Gil. "That is certain. But it was bound to come to this, I suppose, in the end. All that patched up half-baked guesswork witchcraft."

"You watch your tongue, Gil Porter," warned the bonnet.

"I don't necessarily say you," he said. "Though it's as likely you as another of 'em."

"'Tain't, 'tain't," came a muttering from the bonnet. "Proper, I am."

"I'm afraid," said Polly, "that I don't know what anybody's talking about."

"Ah, well," said Gil. "It's a long story. It's to do with a village called Grimstone —"

"I've heard of that!" put in Polly eagerly.

"And how an old woman happened on a book of spells —"

"Me!" croaked the bonnet. "Me! I found it!"

"Found a book of spells," repeated Gil wearily, "and instead of keeping her trap shut, went blabbing all round the village, until next we knew, there was every woman in the place writing down spells and charms and runes — just as if they was recipes, and every one of 'em fancying herself a witch, every one of 'em."

"And then — come May Day — whoosh!" Sam threw up his arms. "Dancing round the maypole, dancing the Gypsy's Tent and — whoosh!"

"What?" cried Polly eagerly. "Whoosh what?"

He shrugged.

"That's just it. There's no-one knows — or least, if they do know, won't tell. Only thing certain is — we slipped the net of time."

"Though there is some rules," said Gil. "Like we can only slip back into time between May Day and Midsummer's Eve."

"And like we can only slip back into time betwixt dawn and sunset," added Sam.

101

"And that we must never touch bread or morsel from the folks in time," said Gil, "else we stop in time for ever."

"Like Baggins!" Polly cried. "Because I fed him!"

"That's it, exact," Gil nodded. "But us — we ain't touched no food, not one of us."

"Not a crumb, not a crumb!" The bonnet now wheeled about. "So why, tell us why, tell us why!" Three times her grimy forefinger stabbed toward Polly.

"Why what?" she faltered.

"Why," said Gil grimly, "*we couldn't get back last even.*"

"Got in the ferry boat same as usual," Sam said. "And into the Time Tunnel, and next thing we knew, we were out the other side — and still *here!*"

"'Twas lucky we'd brought a crust or two with us," said Gil. "Else not even Babby Porter here'd have had never a bite."

"And all night long," said Sam, his voice hushed and fearful, "we lay listening for The Catcher!"

"Every snap, every rustle!" shrieked Granny Porter. "Shiver and shake from dusk to dawn, aches and pains and screws in the joints!"

"I'm sorry, I really am," cried Polly. "But I can't think it's anything to do with me!"

Gil heaved a deep sigh.

"Aye, well," he said, "they'll maybe manage to get us out. They'll be babbling and casting around down there, every woman jill of 'em, and maybe one of 'em'll hit on a way."

"Whist!" hissed the old woman. "There's one of the rules you ain't told." She lowered her voice and thrust her head nearer to Gil's. "You know the one!"

"Ah!" He shook his head. "Only *think* that's a rule,

Granny. It's not certain."

"I'll tell her," Sam said. "But just a minute, first." He got to his feet and moved a few yards away from them among the trees.

"Baggins — here!"

Immediately Boz-Baggins ran to him and stood wagging his tail.

"There!" he said triumphantly. "See that?"

"Boz!" called Polly, jealous. Back he ran.

"See?" she said to Sam.

"Came to me of his own free will," said Sam deliberately. He was not talking to Polly, but to the others.

"Aye, he did," Gil agreed.

"He goes to anyone, if they call him," said Polly defensively.

Gil looked her straight in the eye.

"We *think*," he said slowly, "think, mind you, that if one living being from above earth would come willing with us into the Time Tunnel, then we should be back in Grimstone again."

"Try the dog! We'll try the dog!" screeched Granny Porter.

Polly stepped back quickly.

"No!" she cried. "No, you shan't!"

She looked at the three faces, and was frightened by the intentness she read there. She spun on her heels and fled, calling "Boz! Boz!"

He raced ahead of her, and she heard shouts behind, "Baggins! Baggins!" and knew that the others were in pursuit.

And so Polly Flint fled blindly through her kingdom, as eager now to escape the Time Gypsies as she had ever been to pursue them.

Chapter 6

Once she was safely back, Polly's conscience began to nag. She kept seeing glimpses of the Time Gypsies' faces, tired and white, and even, in Sam's case, scared.

"And poor little Babby Porter," she thought. "Will he die, I wonder, if he don't get back?"

She asked herself this and a hundred other questions, and did not know the answers to any of them.

"There are times," she thought, "when I think I ought to stop meddling with time!" — and the relentlessly counting clock in the hall seemed to echo the thought.

Every now and then she wondered whether it *was* all her fault, but each time pushed the thought away.

"Not my fault. None of it — all the fault of them silly women, trying to be witches, when they're not!"

All the same she plucked up courage to say to Aunt Em when she came to say goodnight: "Aunt Em... I know it's a silly question. But has.... has there ever been any witches in the family?"

Aunt Em drew a very heavy sigh.

"I sometimes wonder," she said wearily, "I really do, whatever daft notion you'll come up with next. No. There has not. And nor will there ever be, there being no such things, as you know as well as I."

"No, Aunt Em," said Polly, and was for once pleased with her aunt's reply.

"Nowt to do with *me*, then," she thought, as she settled herself to sleep. "And they're not even my friends, not really. They wanted to take Boz — and they shan't!"

But she could not sleep. She kept picturing the Time Gypsies out there somewhere in the dark, spending a second night away from home, trying to sleep, but listening for every tiny sound that might mean the approach of The Catcher.

"It'll be pitch dark," she thought, "and owls hooting, and all the little creatures scurrying out from under the banks. And they can't escape. They're prisoners in time." And then she thought, "Dad — he's a prisoner, too. He's just as much a prisoner as them, lying there in that high white bed, never to walk and never to fish."

When at last she fell asleep she dreamed. She dreamed that as the Time Gypsies lay sleeping, that terrible shadowy figure of The Catcher came striding through the woods and discovered them. And how he netted them — first Babby Porter, and then the others, one by one. And as he netted them he threw them into that barred dungeon deep in the woods, and gloated as they cried, "Let us out! Let us out!"

In there, too, were all the other timeless children, the May Dancers, who had played hide and seek with her among the trees, and danced in her honour.

"Let us out, let us out!" they pleaded.

And then, incredibly, another face appeared behind the grille, and it was that of Tom, vainly trying to wrest the iron bars apart as the children flapped vainly about him like imprisoned butterflies.

"Poor little things! Poor little things!" Polly woke crying, and her cheeks were wet with tears.

For a time she lay there, remembering it all. Then, as she came slowly to, she became aware of a light, soft pattering, a rustling and whispering. She knelt up to draw back the curtain, and saw the window beaded with rain. It was falling steadily in the early grey light, and spattered in puddles that already lay black or silver as the light struck them.

"Oh no!" she gasped, dismayed. "They've been out all night, in this!"

She dressed rapidly and went down, sticking out her tongue at the maddening clock as she passed it. Aunt Em already sat at the table, sipping tea.

"Good morning, Aunt Em," she said.

"Not very," she returned. "There's a letter on your plate."

Polly opened it.

"Dear Poll," she read, "you'll know this writing as your mother's, but the words are mine. I'm still lying here the wrong way up, but now the doctors have done something, and they think I will be better. To stand, I mean, Poll, and to walk again..."

She read no further.

"Aunt Em!" she cried. "He's going to walk! Dad's going to walk!"

"Well, I should be pleased to think so," said Aunt Em, who was not easily moved to joy, nor indeed any strong emotion. "But don't go counting chickens. Only *might*, it says in my letter."

"But he will," said Polly stubbornly. "I know my Dad."

She read on.

"You'll have to take me then to that lake of yours, and I can maybe tell you the names of some of them birds of yours. I've still got my own birds in my own head, and always shall, I hope, but it'll be a right pleasure to see some real ones."

Aunt Em's voice interrupted.

"You'll not be thinking of going down Rufford in all this wet?"

"Oh, I shall!" said Polly swiftly. "I get a big enjoyment in rain!"

"Then you've a different idea of enjoyment from mine."

"But what I thought was," said Polly, launching her plan, "that I'd go round knocking some more with the pram, first. There's lots of houses not done yet."

"But the stuff'd get wet," objected Aunt Em.

"Not if I lay something over it," said Polly. "And I could take an umbrella. We collected some umbrellas first time round."

Aunt Em hesitated. Polly held her breath, and listened to the clock. The success of her scheme depended on the answer.

"It would be a help," Aunt Em admitted. "And I suppose a spot of rain won't do any harm, at your age."

"Oh, thank you, Aunt Em!" cried Polly joyously. Aunt Em looked startled at this reaction.

So Polly, wearing her oilskins, set off round the village, pushing the enormous pram, and Boz trotted by her side. Aunt Em had been dubious about allowing this, given the probable state of his paws when he returned, and had finally agreed, Polly guessed, because she was nervous of being left alone with him.

Polly enjoyed knocking on doors and making her request.

"What we *particularly* want," she said at each house, "are warm clothes, rugs or blankets, and umbrellas."

Then she would add, "It's for a very good cause."

And so it was, of course. It was, in her opinion, for a much better cause than the W.I... At many houses she was told what a good girl she was to work so hard,

107

especially in the rain, and given biscuits, sweets and chocolates. These she pushed into her pockets.

The rain came faster. Polly pushed up a big old umbrella that was not without leaks, but served to keep the contents of the pram relatively dry. Nobody was about, it seemed a ghost village. Even the bench by the Red Lion was empty. But she did see Davey Cole. He had a catapult, and was aiming at the maypole.

"Wouldn't do that if he knew what I know," thought Polly.

He looked up, saw her, and stared.

"Look at that!" he shouted to the deserted green. "What you got in there? Rags and bones?"

Polly looked straight ahead and walked on.

"Rags and bones may break your bones, but words will hurt you never," she quoted inaccurately to herself.

"Polly Flint, always skint! Polly Flint, always skint!" he yelled after her.

"Lot *he* knows about rhyming!" she thought. Then she heard the shrill voice of a woman, and looked back over her shoulder to see Davey being called back into the house by his mother.

This was very fortunate for Polly, because she wanted no witnesses for what was to happen next. She looked over her shoulders, left and right. A car splashed by. She began rapidly to push the pram beyond the last house in the village and towards the ford that she would have to cross to reach Rufford.

The wooden footbridge was too narrow for the pram, so Polly had to push it through the ford, the water perilously near the top of her wellingtons. She needed both hands to force the wheels against the weight of the water, so balanced the umbrella precariously on top of the pram.

Then she was over. She ran the few remaining yards with the umbrella swaying wildly, and then was within the shelter of the trees.

She stood for a moment debating with herself which direction to take. She decided that as the tunnel that ran through the largest island was their only lifeline, the Time Gypsies would not have strayed far out of sight of it.

She pushed the pram up the lakeside path, and began to walk towards the island. And as she did so, she slowly became aware that never before had her world been quite so particularly secret, and hers and hers alone. The rain dripped steadily from bough to earth, the surface of the lake was pewter and puckered, all its reflections gone. And as she gazed ahead, blinking through the rain, it seemed to Polly that she could herself at this very moment have gone hundreds of years back in time, and never would know it. There was not one thing, one single sign, to tell her that she was in the twentieth century. Trees, water, birds floating and flying, whitish sky and silvery fall of rain — all were timeless, unchanging, usual as the very air she breathed.

So strongly did this thought come upon her, that she actually stopped, and searched the distances for some sign that she had not herself somehow and by some haphazard magic slipped the net of time. With relief she saw the metallic tower of a pylon, and the reassuring lines of wires. She walked on.

She stopped level with the Time Tunnel and could see straight through to the other side, despite the curtain of rain. Then, out of nothing, appeared the shape of a boat, of figures rowing. It came out of the murky tunnel and into the wide daylight, Polly was witnessing in reverse the very magic she had seen the day before. On impulse, she pulled the pram off the path and in among the trees, and crouched there beside it, one hand on Boz's chain. She heard only the steady pattering of rain, and then, faintly, the creak of rowlocks, the splash of oars.

Craning, she watched as the little boat drew in to the bank. Two children clambered out — bare armed, bare legged in the rain, wearing only the little ragged tunics she had seen them in on the day they had danced for her, by the Silver Pool. They made fast the boat, took from it a small bundle, and disappeared from view.

Polly straightened up. She looked at the pram and hesitated. Then her eye fell on Boz.

"Stay!" she commanded in a whisper. "Stay — and guard!"

She walked away. There was no telltale clink of chain that would have meant Boz was following her.

"I *knew* he could do anything I told him," she thought. "Told that Davey Cole so!"

She moved from tree to tree, always alert for sound or movement. She caught a glimpse of bluish grey, and then the flash of limbs. From where she hid she watched the two children noiselessly flitting back the way they had come, toward the lake.

Polly was torn between following them, watching them row out and witnessing again that strange vanishing under that magical arch, and searching for the stranded trio who were surely hidden somewhere near.

"I'll go back and get Boz and the pram," she decided. "Then watch 'em go. 'Tain't every day you see folks disappear. Then go and find others. Best of both worlds."

She found Boz still sitting patiently by the laden pram.

"You needn't ever think," she told him, "I'll let them Time Gypsies have *you*."

The pair stood side by side watching the little boat swing to enter that mysterious no-man's-land that lay greenish and silent beyond the mouth of the tunnel.

"No man's water," murmured Polly. And then the boat vanished.

> *"Under the tunnel of time they go*
> *To the secret village way below."*

Slowly she shook her head, and turned her back on the lake to scan the woods. Pushing her way through soaked foliage she found the hollow where yesterday they had hidden.

"Gone from there," she thought. "But not much farther off, I should think. Not far from that tunnel."

She was right. The Time Gypsies had evidently been alerted to her approach by the unwieldy and noisy presence of the pram.

"Baggins! Here — Baggins!"

Polly, loosening her hold on the pram handle, saw Sam's face peering from a nearby thicket, disembodied, like that of the Cheshire cat. She raced after Boz-Baggins, terrified that he might be kidnapped — or dognapped — and used as a kind of time hostage by the desperate trio.

She burst into the clearing where the Time Gypsies had hidden themselves. It had at first sight a curiously homelike and sheltered look. A large, whitish outcrop of rock formed one solid wall, the others being of tightly interlaced boughs and undergrowth. The overhanging trees formed a roof of sorts. All this Polly took in only as an impression, there being no opportunity for a closer inspection.

Granny Porter was up in arms in the instant.

"That dog!" she shrieked. "Lay hold of that tricksy creature, can't you, Gil? Catch him! Catch him!"

Boz was jumping joyously and unafraid around Sam and Gil, and Polly felt a pang.

"He *has* been theirs," she thought, "wherever or whenever they found him."

She advanced into the clearing and stood awkwardly, hardly knowing how to manage the encounter.

"It's only me," she said unnecessarily. "Are you all right?"

"We're managing," said Gil.

"That we ain't!" shrilled Granny Porter. "The things you say! I ain't been wuss in years — I ain't been wuss in *hundreds* of years!"

Here she fixed Polly with a challenging glare.

"Let's see what we have here," Gil said. "This'll maybe cheer you, Granny."

She snorted, to indicate the unlikelihood of any such thing, and shuffled and shrugged within her tattered plumage. Gil, meanwhile, was unwrapping a cloth-bound bundle that Polly recognised as the one the children had brought out of the boat. The folds fell away to reveal a round, crusty loaf, a lump of cheese, some flat brown scones or pancakes, eggs, and two earthenware flagons.

Sam, at any rate, cheered visibly. He reached out for the loaf, tore a piece away, and began to ram it into his mouth, at the same time breaking off morsels of cheese and stuffing them in after.

Almost simultaneously out grabbed a grimy, leather-mittened hand, and Granny Porter was feeding with the same greed and rapidity. The pair of them sat with bulging cheeks and smacking lips, and Polly watched and wondered what Aunt Em would make of their table manners. Gil, meanwhile, uncorked the stoneware flagons, and sniffed at each.

"Cider!" he said, and then, "Milk! Come you on here, then, Babby Porter!" He reached and picked up the baby and put the narrow neck of the jar to his lips. A noisy sucking ensued. The Porters were, Polly decided, the noisiest eaters she had ever encountered.

As she stood watching this strange feast, a sudden thought struck her. She put a hand in either pocket and pulled out the haul of goodies she had saved from her rounds.

"Here!" She held them out. "Look — you can have 'em! Biscuits, look, and chocolate, and —"

She broke off. Granny Porter, her cheeks still bulging, and rendered incoherent by crumbs, was making muffled noises and stabbing her finger towards Polly's outspread palms. At last, as the rest watched, mystified, she swallowed hard and screamed.

"Ware crusts! Ware crumbs! Ware goodies!"

Then Polly remembered. "Take neither crust nor crumb from mortal hand."

"Oh!" She clenched her fists and snatched them back. Slowly she loosened them, and the contents fell to the ground, where Boz took a lively interest in them.

"I'm sorry — I forgot! I never meant —"

"Want you ever to get back?" Granny Porter, ignoring Polly, was leaning toward Sam, who was still made speechless by quantities of bread and cheese, and merely nodded vigorously in reply.

"She's slippery!" hissed Granny Porter. "She's

cunning!"

"I'm not! Look!" Polly looked about her and then stamped, vigorously and deliberately, on the scattered sweets and biscuits. "I forgot, didn't I? Anyone can forget. I never meant —"

"How she got the dog," said Gil slowly.

"And how she means to get *us*!" Sam supplied, through a mouth now miraculously emptied.

Polly looked at them, all three.

"I *never* meant that," she said at last. "I never meant anything, except to be friends. *I* don't belong here, any more than you do. And all I wanted —"

She broke off. She felt the rise of shaming tears.

"*Anyway*," she said. "Look at these, and see if you want 'em!"

She pushed her way out of the clearing to where stood the laden pram, umbrellas hanging rakish and askew. It looked so unlikely, so absolutely foreign among all the wild greenery that she giggled, despite herself.

"Jumble!" she said. "For the W.I.!" And then, "Women's Institute — or Witches' Institute!"

With difficulty she manoeuvred the pram under the spreading boughs. As she and it burst together into the secret clearing all three Time Gypsies, their hunger now evidently satisfied, looked towards her, with gratifying interest and astonishment.

"There!" exclaimed Polly triumphantly. "What do you think of *that*?"

The ensuing silence seemed to indicate that they thought little — or nothing — of that. Their looks expressed only extreme mystification.

"It's all for *you*!" cried Polly. "For while you're stuck up here, in the wood. Look!"

And she started to toss the items from the pram,

114

one by one.

"Rug — blanket — got a few holes, but it don't matter — another rug — cushion — what's this? Oh, dressing gown — that'll be handy. Another rug, umbrella, umbrella, umbrella. Might have holes, but all the rain can't come in through them. Another cushion — ever so comfy you can be now!"

She paused. The pram was empty now, and the Time Gypsies were surveying her with unwinking — but uncomprehending — gaze. She looked back at them.

"Oh, don't look at me so!" she half sobbed. "Can't you see I'm on your side?"

"*Them*," said Granny Porter, jerking her head towards the heap of jumble on the ground, "is home things, living things, *stopping* things."

"And we ain't stopping!" Sam cried. "We ain't!"

"But they'll do till you get back," said Polly. "You can be warm and comfy."

"What's warm, what's comfy?" snapped Granny Porter. "And what's *those*!"

She gestured towards the heap, then got up, slowly and complainingly. She shuffled over to the pile and picked up an umbrella. She twirled it, this way and that, held it aloft, where it was poised for an instant, and then brought it down — thwack — on a bed of nettles.

"Not a wand," she said to herself, "not a wand — but what?"

"Look — I'll show you!"

Polly picked up another umbrella. The others watched as she pushed it open.

"Magic!" exclaimed Sam, in awe.

"*No!*" cried Polly. "To keep the rain off — look!"

She held the umbrella above her head, and the

heavy drops of rain that penetrated the roof of over-hanging trees spattered heavily and noisily upon it.

"Keep Babby Porter dry!" she said, and placed the opened umbrella over him, where he lay, wide eyed and placid after his recent feed.

"There!" Polly turned toward her audience. "He'll be kept dry now, you see."

"I do believe he will," said Gil slowly.

"Sticks isn't *meant* to open out like mushrooms!" Granny Porter was not to be won over thus easily. "*I've* never see a stick open out, I never!"

"There's one here." Sam picked another from the heap. "Is this one?"

"I'll show you," offered Polly eagerly. And she pushed his finger up so that the umbrella unfurled, and he looked disbelievingly up at the multi-coloured spread of it, and was clearly enchanted by it, and began to caper about, crying, "It's a rain shield, it's a rain shield!"

"Umbrella," said Polly.

"Umbrella," he echoed, "a rain shield umbrella!"

"Hist you and hush you up!" Granny Porter was on her feet now, dodging back and forth to wrench the handle from his grasp. "Let it go, let it go — there!"

She tugged it from his hand, and as she did so, a spoke bent and broke.

"No — oh, now you've broke it!"

"Never mind," said Polly. "I've got another — and another."

She pulled them from the pile to prove it. But again a silence and a wariness had fallen upon the Time Gypsies.

"Safe from rain," said Gil. "But it's not rain that threatens."

They looked at him then, all three, while Babby

116

Porter, forgotten, gazed at his bright new canopy.

"Time that threatens," said Gil. "What's to keep us safe from time?"

"And The Catcher," put in Sam.

"Oh, what'll become of us, what'll become of us." Granny Porter rocked back and forth, dismal and fraught.

"I wish I'd never come!" burst out Sam. "I wish I'd stopped and never come out of Grimstone at all!"

"*That's* not true, Sam," said Gil. "All the children come into time, at the May Dancing. Like moths to the flame the children run, century in and century out."

"Is that true?" asked Polly, wondering. "Do you always come? Every May Day there has been?"

"Always," he replied. "Leastways, always the children. It's part of the spell — or seems to be."

"I think it's a marvellous magic," Polly said, "for a village to be there, way down below, and the children dancing and the bells ringing — and do you know, I've heard them bells, heard 'em, with my own ears!"

"And so you might," nodded Gil, "for ring they do."

"But my Aunt Em don't hear them," said Polly, "and nobody else, that I know of. My Aunt Em don't even believe you're there!"

"Then your Aunt Em's a silly old woman!" said Sam.

"*She'd* never believe you could skip in and out of time," Polly said. "And she's got a clock, a great big clock, and all day long and all night long it ticks the loudest tick you've ever heard — tick tock tick tock till it nearly drives me silly!"

They were listening now, intent and unsmiling.

"My Aunt Em," Polly went on, encouraged, "is the biggest believer in time I have ever met. And that

117

clock — the one I told you about — has never lost *one single second*! Can you believe it?"

"A Catcher," Gil looked uncertainly at the others. Another Catcher?"

"Oh, she's not *magic*!" Polly cried. "Not Aunt Em! She sat right next to you," turning to Granny Porter, "and never even knew!"

"I never said magic," Gil said. "I said Catcher."

"Who — who is The Catcher?" Polly was timid now, treading on dangerous ground. "I think I've seen him — I know I have, striding, with a great net. But why does he come? Why does he —?"

"The Catcher," said Gil, "is the one who comes and who would have us all trapped in the net of time. As long as we run free — as long as the children of Grimstone run free as they do, in and out of days, in and out of years —"

"Then he'll *snatch*!" screamed Granny Porter. "He'll run and he'll chase and he'll *snatch*, till he has us all tangled again in the net of time!"

"I think I see," said Polly Flint slowly. "I think I've been seeing for a long time now — ever since I saw that angel. I saw a coal miner as well, for that matter, and I saw things in the fields there back home, and heard voices in the woods. And now I'm seeing you, and I know you're real, and a million Aunt Ems couldn't tell me you're not."

She looked round and saw that all three of them, except Babby Porter, of course, were listening, really listening for perhaps the first time since she had met them.

"In fact," she finished, "my Aunt Em is so locked up in time, so trapped, she can't see and she can't hear and she don't believe *owt*!"

"Could it," said Gil, "could it be that her *clock* has

118

us caught?"

Granny Porter shook her head to and fro.

"If you think it is," said Polly, "I'll stop it, I will. Though I daresay she'd kill me, when she found out."

Sam suddenly stood up.

"I reckon I like her," he said, meaning Polly. He looked directly at her. "It's not your fault. I know it's not."

"Oh thank you!" cried Polly. "Thank you!"

"There's no need playing silly sweethearts!" snapped Granny Porter.

"Shall you come for a walk alonger me?" Sam asked Polly.

"Oh yes, yes!"

"You stop 'em, Gil," ordered Granny Porter.

"I shan't stop 'em," said Gil. "No harm to be done."

As Polly and Sam pushed their way out of the clearing they could hear Granny Porter's complaining croon.

"No harm done, but harm to come... no harm done, but harm to come..."

The voice faded. They stopped, looked at one another, and smiled.

"Don't she rattle!" said Sam. "Don't she just *rattle*!"

"Worse than my Aunt Em," said Polly. "And I never thought anybody could be that."

They walked on a little through the drenched woods, and there was a healing silence. Only the birds spoke, and the trees.

"Wish my Mam was here," said Sam, at length.

"Your Mam?" Polly was taken aback. "Oh — I didn't know! I thought —"

"Down there, still," he said mournfully. "Never came up with us. Said she'd milking to do."

119

Polly looked at the beautifully calm and reflecting lake and thought, "Think — *cows* under there! Not reflecting cows, but proper — with milk to give!"

Aloud, she said, "*Shall* you ever get back, do you think?"

"Oh, don't say that!" He was aghast. "Don't say it!"

"I'd help you," Polly said. "Any way I could. And my Mam and Dad, when they get back. They would."

They were climbing the stone steps that led to the wide lawns in front of the Abbey. Here and there were stone statues and urns, and Polly caught sight of two slight figures mounted and swaying on a plinth.

"Oh — look!"

Sam followed her pointing finger.

"It's Tommy and Jess!"

He began to race off towards them. Polly felt cut off. She was in one world, she felt, and he in another. She saw then, on a seat nearby, a woman with an easel, painting. As Polly watched, the woman looked up, directly at the statue where Tommy and Jess were entwined, and then back to her canvas.

"That statue..." Polly thought. "She's painting that statue..."

She looked at the Time Gypsies, waving now toward the approaching Sam, and then again at the painter.

"Does she see 'em? Chance to find out... After all, ain't *sure* Aunt Em didn't see Granny Porter..."

Polly advanced slowly towards the artist, and just then she looked up, saw Polly, and smiled.

"Can I look?" Polly asked, and it was the hugest question she had ever asked in her life.

The woman nodded.

Polly approached and looked, half expectant, half fearful. What she saw was a painting of the lawn and trees beyond, and the very statue where now the Time Gypsies were swaying and climbing, but not a sign of any human being.

"It's very good," Polly said.

"Thank you."

"Er — didn't you want to put them in, then?"

"Put what in, dear?"

"I mean — well — don't you bother putting people in?" Polly was hard put to frame her question tactfully. "I'm not very good at drawing people, either."

The woman laughed.

"If there were any to *put* in!"

Polly heard voices and laughter and looked back toward the statue, to see that now dozens of Time Gypsy children — or so it seemed — were converging on the statue from all sides. Some of them danced and fiddled as they came, others ran ahead to form a ring about the statue.

"She don't see them," Polly thought. "Or hear them. She really don't. And what *that* means, is that they *ain't* here even if they *are*..."

She shook her head.

"You work *that* out, Polly Flint!" she told herself. At that moment Sam cupped his hands to his mouth and bawled, "Baggins! Baggins! Here!"

Boz-Baggins tore off over the wide lawn, haloed in a spray of raindrops.

"What has your dog seen, I wonder?" said the artist, startled. "A rabbit, perhaps."

"I expect so," Polly agreed. "He's very keen on rabbits."

But to herself, she thought, "Rummest-looking lot of rabbits *I've* ever seen!"

She watched as Boz-Baggins ran from one Time Gypsy to the other, wagging his tail and even jumping up.

"He really is behaving very oddly," she heard the woman say.

"Oh! Oh — he's always like that. Daft as a brush! I'll go and fetch him. Thanks for letting me see your painting. Goodbye!"

She started off to join the others, but as she approached the Time Gypsies scattered as swiftly as they had assembled, and by the time she reached the statue, only Sam was left.

"Why've they all run off?" she asked.

Sam shrugged.

"Scared."

"Of *me*?"

"You can see 'em, see. They ain't used to that. Taken *me* some getting used to. And with us four getting stuck, they think it's to do with you."

"I keep telling you, it's not!"

"I dunno," Sam said. "Not o' purpose you didn't, anyhow."

Polly became aware of voices again, and laughter, and she turned to see that the Time Gypsy children were crowding around the artist and her easel, while she painted on, oblivious.

"Just you look at *that*!" Polly exclaimed. "And hark at the noise, blowing through leaves! It's as hard for me as it is for you. I can't *believe* that she don't see and hear them!"

"Would you help?" asked Sam suddenly. "Really help?"

"Of course, I want to."

"Not just bringing blankets, and such," he said. "Really help."

122

Polly glanced sideways at him, and saw how serious he was.

"What do you mean?" Shc was half fearful.

"What Granny Porter said yesterday... about someone from above earth going willingly into the Time Tunnel..."

"Oh!" Polly gasped. "I don't know if I'd dare! What if I couldn't get back — then I'd be stuck, same as you! I'd have to stop in Grimstone for ever and ever!"

"I could marry you," he said simply. "You'd be all right."

Polly laughed delightedly, and then saw his hurt expression and immediately straightened her face.

"I'm not laughing at you," she said, "really I'm not. It's just the idea! And what about my Mam and Dad? They've only got me."

But Sam had gone stamping on ahead.

"Leave it!" his voice came. "We'll *live* under a bush all our lives, that's all!" He paused. "Not even all our lives — till The Catcher gets us!"

Polly ran and caught up with him, seizing her chance.

"And what will happen if he does?"

"Nobody knows. There's tales flown here and there for hundreds of years." He lowered his voice. "There's some says that the minute that net drops over your head — pouff — you're gone! Gone to a pile of dust!"

"Oh no!" Polly was aghast.

"And there's others say that if once he nets a Time Gypsy, we're all finished, every one of us. It'll put all Grimstone under his spell, and —"

"Look!" Polly pointed toward the lake.

Sam followed the direction of her finger. There

were four little boats crossing steadily from bank to island.

"What of it?" he said. He added bitterly, "Going back, *they* are."

"But there's four boats! Boats aren't allowed. Why don't the keeper stop 'em?"

"Because he don't *see* 'em, of course."

"Don't see the children, I know that. But the boats!"

"You still don't understand, do you?" said Sam wearily.

Polly shook her head. Evidently she did not.

"Look," he told her, "the lake's the same place for you and us. Only the *time* that's different."

Polly stared.

"Of course!"

And she seemed to hear again Old Mazy's voice: "Water always finds its own level..."

When they returned to the clearing, Granny Porter's mood had not improved.

"She let you back, then?" she snapped.

"I saw the others, some of 'em," Sam told her. "They'd messages."

"Messages?" screeched Granny Porter. "Messages? *They'll* not get us out!"

"Mam says to make sure Babby's his crust to chew on," Sam told Gil. "And says not to lose heart."

"I've lost heart," moaned Granny Porter, rocking her raggedy person to and fro. "Gone to turnip, my heart has. Drat that babby, drat it!"

Babby Porter had woken up and was crying again.

"It's all wickedness and woe, wickedness and woe! You can stand there, oh yes, all very well for you. You ain't stuck from home, and like to be for ever, oh no!"

124

"Yes I am, then!" cried Polly. "I *am* stuck away from home, *and* on my own. I've got sad things in my life, as well as you! And my dad was in an accident, and can't walk, and that's worse than *anything* that's happened to you!"

"There's no use your rattling on," said Granny Porter. "My old head don't work when that babby's bawling."

Polly had an inspiration.

"Shall I take him a walk?" she asked. "In the pram?"

They looked mystified.

"In that." She pointed. "That's what it's for, really. Pushing babies in. It rocks them, and they go to sleep."

"You could run off with him," said Granny Porter. "Or feed him, like you did that dog."

"Oh I wouldn't, you know I wouldn't! Look — I'll leave Boz here with you, if you like — Baggins. Then you'll know I'll come back."

"She would, Granny," said Sam. "She wouldn't lose her dog for *that* squally lump."

"Go on, then!" she snapped. "Get off, get off!"

She turned her back. Sam picked up his fiddle and started to play, a slow, sad tune. Gil was staring into space as if in a dream.

"All right, I will!"

No-one replied. The bow pulled mournful notes from the strings.

So Polly lined the pram with a rug, pulled out a cushion from the pile, and picked up Babby Porter, still squalling.

"You *are* a lump!" she told him, as she pulled the rug over him. Then, to the others, "I shan't be very long. Just long enough to get him back to sleep. Boz — stay!"

"He's all right," said Sam, without pause from his fiddling. "Come on, then, Baggins old lad."

Polly enjoyed pushing the pram now that it had a baby in it.

"Wonder how many hundreds of years old you are," she mused. "And another thing I wonder. If I was to meet somebody — would they see you and hear you? If not, they'd think I was plain daft, walking along and talking to an empty pram!"

The rain had stopped now and the sun came out so that the soaked grass and every leaf of every tree flashed and glittered. Polly's spirits rose.

"It ain't such a bad old world," she told Babby Porter. "My Dad's going to walk again, for practically certain positive! You might even get to see him, if he comes here soon!"

Babby Porter looked neither pleased nor displeased at this prospect. He simply lay and gazed up into Polly's face, and she found herself flattered by this.

"Least *you* like me," she told him, after a time.

"And as for old Granny Porter, bet she don't like anybody. Same with my Aunt Em. Proper battleaxe she is."

But Babby Porter was not listening. His eyes were closed and he was breathing peacefully. Polly gave herself the entire credit for this, and carefully turned the pram to retrace her steps.

A shadow fell across the pram. Polly gave a little shriek and clapped a hand to her mouth. She was looking up into the smiling face of Old Mazy.

"Oh! You made me jump!" Her mind was working rapidly. Could he — would he — see the slumbering Babby Porter in the depths of the big hood?

"Giving someone a push, are you?" he asked.

Polly took a deep breath.

126

"Oh no! Don't even *know* any babbies — babies, I mean. Just some old rugs and that, for the jumble."

He stooped from his enormous height and peered in. Polly held her breath. He straightened up again.

"You'll not collect a deal in *these* parts," he observed, eyeing her closely. "Not many doors to knock on here."

Polly's legs felt silly with relief. She started to push the pram on.

"Just having a bit of a walk, that's all," she called over her shoulder. "Got sick of collecting."

He did not reply. Polly dared not turn her head at first, and when at last she did, he had disappeared.

"Not following me, then," she thought. "Don't even know he is The Catcher, anyhow. Not for sure."

She hummed a little under her breath as she approached the clearing where the Time Gypsies were encamped. At last, she felt, they trusted her. They would never otherwise have let her go off with Babby Porter.

She pushed aside the overhanging leaves and was stung by a cold spray.

"Hallo!" she called. "Hallo! It's me!"

There was no reply. She was right through the thicket now. Her heart gave a tremendous lurch. The clearing was empty.

"Boz!" she called. "Boz — here!"

She looked about her and saw that the pile of rugs was still there, and the cushions and umbrellas and oddments of clothing.

"Where are they?" She spoke out loud. Then, "Oh! Oh no! The Catcher!"

She had a swift picture of that shadowy figure, net upraised. Old Mazy was abroad in the wood, that she knew.

"But he didn't see Babby Porter — least, didn't seem to."

She stood bewildered.

"Oh, where are you?" she cried desperately. "Where *are* you?"

She heard only the spattering of moisture from the soaked foliage.

"Lake's most likely," she thought. "I'll look. Can't leave *him* here, though. And can't go very fast, either, pushing that great pram."

For a moment she hesitated. Then she reached and picked up the pinkly slumbering Babby Porter, and began to run, through the thicket, past the bluebell acres and down to the edge of the lake.

She stood aghast.

"No!" she screamed. "No!"

There, in a wooden rowing boat, was Granny Porter, making for the island and the arch. And there, sitting in the bow like a figurehead, was Boz-Baggins.

Chapter 7

That ferry to another time and another place went heedlessly over that bright water and there was nothing Polly Flint could do to stop it.

She screamed, "Stop! Stop!"

Granny Porter made not a sign. The boat went, slow and implacable, towards that fateful tunnel.

"You're a bad old woman!" Polly screamed. "A bad, wicked old woman! You come back!"

There was no reply. The bundle of tatters topped by the large bonnet was mute. Even Boz did not bark, or make any sign of recognition.

"Lost!" She was almost in tears. "He'll go under that tunnel, and then I'll never see him again!"

It was only Babby Porter's renewed squalling that reminded Polly that she had him — was, indeed, holding him.

"Left holding the baby!" She half smiled through her tears.

An idea struck her.

"You come back this minute," she yelled, "or I'll drop Babby Porter in the lake!"

She held him aloft to demonstrate the seriousness of the threat, but the boat was turning now by the island, only yards away from that eerily green arch.

"I mean it!"

Slowly the boat swung.

"Oh! She can't hear me!" Polly was sobbing in earnest now. "Oh — goodbye, Boz! Goodbye!"

She could not bear to watch. She could not bear to see him dissolve into air, and know him gone beyond call, forever. She turned away, half blinded by tears.

They splashed on to the grubby face of Babby Porter, who cried anew.

"I didn't mean it," she told him, ashamed. "Don't cry. I shan't really drop you in the lake."

She fished for a hanky and dried his face, and then her own. Slowly she turned to face the lake again.

It was deserted, as she had known it would be. Only the wild birds went sailing, making their v-shaped wakes, or dipping and pecking and doing all the other things they did every day of the year. There was no sight, no sound, of the boat that was bearing Granny Porter and Boz-Baggins to another world, another time.

Polly turned and walked slowly away.

"Only had him for a bit," she thought, "but I'll never forget him, never."

Then her mind, numbed with shock, began to work again.

"But I've got him!" looking down at Babby Porter. "And where's the other two — Sam and Gil?"

They must, she decided, be already back in Grimstone.

"Went ahead and took Boz, then sent him back for Granny Porter."

Stunned as she was, she did not stop to wonder how Boz could have brought the boat back alone through the tunnel, and to the waiting Granny Porter on the bank.

"But what about Babby Porter? They'll be back for him, surely! Can't go leaving a baby behind!"

She had reached the clearing, and pushed her way through to where the pram stood.

"You really are a lump," she told Babby Porter as she lowered him into it. "My arms fair *ache*!"

He gazed up at her, content again.

"It's near time for my dinner," she told him. "Must be, by now. My Aunt Em'll be caterwauling. But what'll I do with you? If she do see you, she'll want to know where I got you from, that is for certain positive. You don't go fetching babies home like a bunch of bluebells.

"But if she doesn't see you, she might go dropping a heap of jumble right on top of you!"

Polly began to push the pram out of the thicket with no very clear idea of where she was going, or what she was going to do.

"And you'll get hungry soon," she told him. "And then what'll I do? I'll feed you, then you'll stop in time forever..."

She turned the matter over.

"My Mam and Dad might be pleased — always wanted a lot of children. Only thing is, where will I say I got you from? They'd never believe me, not in a million years. Not even my Dad, and he's a big believer in things. Even believed in my angel..."

She looked again at Babby Porter, cocooned in his grubby bundle.

"But he'd never swallow you!"

He gazed solemnly up at her.

"Crikey — wonder if you need your nappy changing?"

Babby Porter was becoming more of a liability by the minute.

"Oh dear!" Polly was close to tears again. "Don't know what time it is, but it must easily be dinner time. What'll I *do*? Oh, they have landed me! And I thought they was my friends. Thought Sam was, anyhow. They tricked me. They tricked me on purpose! I wish The Catcher *had* got 'em, I do! Serve 'em right!"

She stopped pushing. She had arrived, without

realising it, at the dark corner under the yews where stood the row of little animal graves. She went over and walked along the line.

"'Boris'," she read. "'Faithful friends are hard to find.' Oh, true — that's true it is, and I've lost you now, forever!"

She lifted her head and saw, half blinded by tears, a blurry black shape beyond the railings. She brushed her sleeve across her eyes and stared, incredulous.

There, sitting as he had been that day when she first found him, eyes fixed on her under that tufted fringe — was Boz.

"Oh!" she gasped. "Can't be." And then, joyously, "Boz, Boz!"

Then he was at her feet, tail wagging furiously, licking her hands, and warm, solid and undeniably *there*!

"Oh Boz — I thought I'd lost you! Thought I'd never see you again! But where've you come from? Just saw you go under that tunnel, I did, with that mucky old woman. Can't be in two times at the same time, surely?"

He gazed up at her.

"Oh, if only dogs could speak! Couldn't be a Boz *and* a Baggins, could there? Twins?"

As she pondered the matter, a voice called: "Baggins! Baggins!"

It was Sam's voice, close by. Polly, astounded, scrambled to her feet.

"Here!" she called. "Here, Sam!"

The next minute he was there, torn shirt and breeches and mud-stained face as usual. Polly's mind reeled.

"But I thought — I thought you'd —"

132

"Gone," he supplied. "I know. We heard you screaming."

"But how? Hadn't you gone into the Time Tunnel?"

"Not us," he said. "Only Granny. Couldn't stop her. She'd got Baggins and shoved off before we knew."

"Oh — oh, I'm *glad*!" Polly threw her arms about the startled Sam and kissed him, mud and all.

"Hold on now," he said, bashful and pulling free. "'Tain't mistletoe time!"

"'Tis for me! I can't believe it! I've got Boz back, and now you can take Babby Porter. Where's Gil?"

"Coming. He stopped over the other side of the lake, to wait on the boat coming."

"She went right through that arch, and straight out at the other side!" Polly laughed with delight. "And I never saw, because I had my eyes shut! Couldn't bear to see Boz disappear."

"All right for you to laugh," Sam said. "'Tain't you that's stuck."

"I'm only laughing because I'm glad you didn't trick me. That we're still friends."

"Listen!" Sam told her. "Oh — it's them."

Floating through the trees came the unmistakable voice of Granny Porter.

"Catched in the net, catched and caught! Dear dear oh deary me! Catched in the net, catched and caught and cooked!"

"Now hush you, Granny," they heard Gil say.

"She's a bad old woman, that Granny Porter," said Polly. "She would've got off and taken Boz, if she could."

"She's bad on top," Sam conceded. "But not underneath."

The familiar bunch of walking shrubbery, topped

by its tattered bonnet, was in sight now.

"Here!" Sam called.

The bonnet lifted. Granny Porter's eyes looked straight into Polly's, and the strangest thing happened.

The little grimy fingers in their leather mitts clutched at Gil's sleeve, and the bonnet came down again, and "Oh, she'll scold and scratch, scold and scratch out my eyes! I'm frightened and feared, frightened and feared!"

"Of *me*?" thought Polly Flint. "Can she mean me?"

"I'm a bad old woman, I am, I am," wailed the bobbing bonnet. "I ought to be pelted and pinched and ducked!"

"What does she mean, 'ducked'?" whispered Polly.

"In the lake. Ducking stool."

"But she's old!" Polly was shocked.

Sam shrugged. "Been ducked times a-plenty, she has," he said. "Bound to be — a tongue like hers! 'Sides — the wash don't do her any harm!"

Then, in an instant and a flurry of rags, Granny Porter was right by Polly, clutching at her with her tiny hands.

"Oh deary, oh deary, I'm sorry, I am!" she wailed. "I'm a bad old woman, I am! But don't let 'em duck me!"

"Oh, *poor* Granny Porter!" Polly turned to Gil. "You won't let them, will you?"

He made a gesture that seemed to mean that he had no say in the matter, one way or the other.

"I know I'm bad," whimpered the derelict bonnet. "But I'm an old woman, and I hankered so to be back by my hearth in Grimstone. I'm frit here, frit!"

As Polly stood awkwardly searching for the words to comfort her, she was all at once aware of a stir in

134

the woods.

"Listen!"

She turned left and right and caught glimpses of running children.

"The May Dancers!"

They ran from the trees and encircled the five of them.

"Not lost!" Gil said. "Not yet."

Then they were tugging at his sleeve, pulling him apart from the others, and he allowed himself to be led until he was a little way off. One of them Polly could see was whispering in his ear, while the rest huddled and hovered close about him, they flapping moths and he the flame.

Polly watched them.

"Always secrets, with you," she said. "And me left on the outside."

"Could be a spell!" Granny Porter was all a-twitch again, her tears forgotten. "Could be the way back they've found. Could be cooking little cakes on my own griddle, this very night!"

"And me rabbiting," said Sam hungrily, "with the rest. For the moon's full!"

Hearing them speak so, Polly felt a pang. She had a sudden strong awareness of their other life in Grimstone, their real life.

"For this, up here, is only like a dream to them," she thought.

She could almost see Grimstone as it would be when they came to it at evening, little lamps lit and reflecting in the lake, and owls hooting beyond and the lonely bark of a fox. She could almost smell the delicious warm scent of cakes baking on a griddle, and see the bare, moonlit acres where Sam and his friends would go snaring rabbits and creeping along the black-shadowed hedgerows.

"I hope you *do* get back!" she found herself saying, without really meaning to have said it at all.

"Oooh, it's The Catcher I fear," moaned Granny Porter. "'Tis that net of his that tangles in my dreams."

"I almost think," said Polly slowly, "that I know who he is."

They looked at her, all three, for Gil had now pulled away from the May Dancers. Polly heard again the weird music they made as they blew through leaves, or played their flutes or fiddles.

"I'm not positive certain," she said, "but I think it might be a man in the village they call Old Mazy."

There was an enormous silence.

"Old Mazy!" screamed Granny Porter, with a force that would have blown out candles, had there been any there.

"*Him!*" Sam was incredulous, but not more so than Polly herself.

"You know him?"

"Him that got left," said Granny Porter. "Him that come up after the May Dancing don't know how many centuries back. And was seen in Grimstone never again."

"Must've eaten summat," supplied Sam. "That's what we thought."

"That was afore we knew the rule," Gil said. "It was him getting caught back in time gave us the rule. He was spotted, see, eating a crust a farmer woman gave him."

"But why does he go after you with that net?" Polly was dizzy.

"I reckon," Gil said slowly, "he thinks it's the only road to get back. I reckon he thinks that if he catched a Time Gypsy, he'd get to Grimstone in his place."

"And he needn't!" Polly cried. "You said that if a single person from above earth was to come with you, willingly, then —"

"We'd be home!" shouted Sam. "Whee!" and he spun with such force that he fell to the ground, and the circling children gave a patter of applause.

"Find him!" screeched Granny Porter, dancing madly on the spot and kicking her muddy little boots. "Find The Catcher!"

"Now steady," Gil said. "If we're mistook, we're done for." He addressed Polly. "What do you know of Old Mazy? Why've you got him notched as The Catcher?"

"Because he seems to have known," she said, "right from the start. He told me he could hear the church bells ringing below on any Sabbath — and he told me to listen, and I did, and I heard 'em, too. And it's only him who knows of the Time Gypsies. And my Aunt Em says he only comes to Wellow this time of year — then goes off."

"Betwixt May Day and Midsummer Eve," nodded Gil. "It fits."

"And he said to me that he'd do as he always does — watch and wait."

"It's him!" screeched Granny Porter. "It's The Catcher! Old Mazy, that got hisself catched in the net of time, and couldn't get free! And now he can, he can, he can — and so can we!" She danced a triumphant jig and her rags flew.

"Oh, you're a duck," she told Polly. "Oh, you're a proper little duck of a gel, and haven't I said so, all along!"

"You *never*!" thought Polly, but held her tongue.

"You *never*!" said Sam indignantly on her behalf.

137

"You called her black and blue!"

"Oh, 'twas only a manner of speaking," said Granny Porter blithely.

"The others..." Sam looked towards where the May Dancers were still grouped a little way off. "What do they want?"

"Shouldn't be needed, not now," Gil said. He looked straight at Polly. "They say that the women have worked at that book of spells day and night. And they say that if you was willing to come alonger us, of your own free will, as you'll remember — they was all but certain they could spin you back into time, after."

"How?" Sam demanded.

"The May Dances," said Gil simply. "If she —" jerking his head towards Polly — "was to join in the May Dancing with the rest, we could spin her off into time again."

"But May Day's gone," Sam said.

"They know that," Gil told him, "in Grimstone, same as we know it here. *Despite* of that they reckon they could spin her back. Anyhow, hardly matters now. Old Mazy can work it for us."

"Oh, but what if I could," said Polly softly. "Oh to see it — to see it with my own eyes!"

"Could still," Sam suggested.

"Could I? Could I?"

Gil nodded.

"But there'd be the risk. Of not spinning back."

"Them's daft, patched-up witches down there," said Granny Porter jealously. "Not proper, like I am, they ain't. Don't you go laying store by *their* spells."

> *Who can tell, who can tell —*
> *Will it work, that secret spell?*

The Time Gypsies looked at Polly in surprise.

"Sorry," she said. "Rhyming. I get it off my Dad. Listen, when I get back now, up the village, shall I tell Old Mazy, if he's there?"

The Time Gypsies looked at one another.

"Aye," said Gil, having read those looks. "And our thanks to you for your pains."

"And shall I say tonight?"

"Tonight," Gil nodded. "Before the sun sets."

"And when the moon rises in Grimstone, white and full!" crooned Granny Porter.

"I'll have to go," Polly said. "What's the time?"

They looked askance.

"I haven't got a watch," she explained, and in the instant realised that nor, of course, had they. "Ask a silly question...! Here!" She thrust Babby Porter into Gil's arms. "Take him. I'll have to run!"

She started to run, and the pram rocked wildly.

"Let him be there, let him be there!" she prayed as she ran.

She went so pell mell and so blind that she did not see the hooked stick go out to catch her ankle, and down she went as she had before.

She looked up, and there was the face of Old Mazy, but this time it was not smiling. And this time he put out a hand and wordlessly pulled her to her feet.

They stared into one another's eyes.

Then, "Help me," said Old Mazy. "Help me, won't you?"

Polly nodded.

"You've seen 'em, haven't you? Spoke with 'em. The Time Gypsies?"

Again she nodded.

"And I can't, I can't! The years go by, and every year they're fainter, till now I can glimpse only flickers, see

139

only their shadows and hear only whispers. And I try to catch 'em — for I'm homesick! Centuries' homesick I am to be again in Grimstone."

"I know," said Polly. "And I am going to help you."

He hardly seemed to take in what she said.

"The pain of it," he said, "to wander the world, and belong nowhere. A stranger in time, I am, and without a friend. And year after year I come back for the May Dancing, and year after year I come but a fingertip away... But they slip through my fingers, and through my net, and I'm left alone, and all I have left are dreams of timeless Grimstone, and even they grow cold...."

"Listen," said Polly, and her heart now ached for his loneliness. "They sent me to tell you. They're caught in the net of time themselves, the same as you are — least, four of 'em are. Granny Porter, and —"

"Granny Porter!" Old Mazy was jubilant to hear a well known name. "Her — that old leathery thing, with —"

"Quick!" said Polly. "Yes, her. And they can only get back, they say, if one person from above earth goes willing with them. And they say that's you."

"Go with them? Willing? When all my heart's desire these hundreds of years —"

"I know," Polly told him. "You thought you had to catch one. But you don't."

He was shaking his head back and forth, back and forth, dazed.

"They want to go tonight," she told him.

"Tonight?"

"Before sunset," she said. "You know that."

"Betwixt dawn and sunset we slip the nets of time..." he murmured.

"They say be there," Polly said, "on the bank of the

140

lake, by the Time Tunnel."

"And I shall run free!" he cried. "Free again in time, and back in Grimstone and the lost land!"

"I've to go," Polly said, catching hold again of the pram. "But be there. And... and..." she hesitated, then called over her shoulder, "*I* may be, as well!"

On she went and past the maypole, and she looked up at it as she always did, and thought: "Dare I? Dare I?" and sped on to Forge Cottage and the black looks that awaited her.

Aunt Em cast a cold look over Polly and the almost empty pram.

"And that, I suppose," she said, "has taken you all morning to collect. And half the afternoon, if it comes to that. Have you no idea of time?"

"Know more about time than *you* do," Polly thought. "That *is* for positive certain!"

Aloud she said, "It's with me not having a watch. And I did collect more than this, but it —"

She trailed off, as she realised that it would be impossible to explain to Aunt Em that she had emptied the pram in order to walk a Time Gypsy baby.

"Well, I left it somewhere," she ended lamely. "It — it was too heavy to push, so I left it. But I'll go and fetch it, I will, later on."

"That," said Aunt Em, "you will not. It'll come to no harm between now and tomorrow."

Polly visualised the damp and muddy clearing.

"That," she thought, "is what you think!"

"And you'll not go out again today," continued Aunt Em, ignoring Polly's gasp of dismay. "You'll go in and eat your dinner — which is stone cold. It's stone cold chips and stone cold sausage. Your favourite, Alice told me, and so I made it, though I don't hold with fried food. And now you'll eat it, stone cold. And you'll not set foot out of this house again today."

"But why not?" Polly cried. "I'll eat the stone cold sausages and chips — I like 'em cold, I do, nearly as well as hot. But why can't I go out?"

"Don't you stand there," said Aunt Em, "answering back your elders and betters."

So Polly went through and ate her stone cold meal.

"I'm a younger and worser, I suppose," she thought. "Why does getting older make you better?"

By mid-afternoon Aunt Em's mood seemed to have improved. She and Polly went into the garden and picked flowers, and arranged them in vases which they then stood about the house.

"They're lovely," Polly said. "Anyone'd think it was someone's birthday!

Aunt Em seemed pleased with this remark.

"I'm going to make tarts now," she said. "Should you like to help?"

So Polly, still hoping for a reprieve, still hoping that she would be released before the day ended, helped with the tarts, and became remarkably floury in the process. She was also caught in the act of licking a spoonful of jam.

"Licking's dirty," said Aunt Em. "Polly — *don't*!"

"Shall I *ever* be Polly do?" she wondered.

"Hmmm!" Once the oven door was shut, Aunt Em turned her attention to Polly. "A fine sight you look. Get upstairs, and change into something decent. Haven't you got a nice frock?"

Polly trudged up to her room and dutifully changed into her best frock. She opened the window and leaned out and smelt the delicious May scent of grass and approaching dewfall, and stared in awe at the towering maypole.

142

> *"A maypole in the month of May*
> *Is magical, or so they say..."*

She murmured the rhyme softly.

"Aunt Em can't kill me," she told the maypole. "If she did, the police would get her. And I've made my mind up. I dare go into the tunnel. I'd dare anything, almost, to be out of time and in Grimstone with the Time Gypsies. Never, never in my whole life again I'll get the chance to be out of time and running free. I'm coming, never fear. I'm coming!" She shut the window, straightened her face and her frock, and went back downstairs.

"Very nice," said Aunt Em, casting an eye over her. "You can do very well, Polly, if you try."

"All I've to do," thought Polly, "'is wait my chance — and run!"

She looked out at the square framed view of the sky from the window, and tried to judge how far away sunset was. The clock in the hall was no help at all at telling this particular kind of time.

"You'll have to stop, Boz," she whispered to him. "Daren't take you. You might end up as Baggins again!"

Meanwhile she sat and listened to the clock in the hall making time seem so dense and actual that she almost felt she could touch it. Aunt Em seemed fidgety — excited, even.

Polly had an unexpected stroke of luck. The telephone rang. Aunt Em came in and said that she had to go out for a few minutes, to a neighbour.

"I shan't be long," she promised. "You look after the house while I'm gone."

The front door shut. Polly was instantly ready to go.

143

"There'll be no-one run off with the house," she told the grandfather clock, as she waited to give Aunt Em time to disappear, "but with any luck, someone'll run off with *you*!"

She peered cautiously about the green. No-one was in sight but the ubiquitous Davey Cole.

"Where're you going?" he called. "I could come with you!"

"Not now!" she called back. "Meeting somebody else!"

With that she was gone to the unclocked, uncharted, uncertain place that awaited her — to Grimstone. The sun was already beginning to set as she crossed the ford and entered Rufford, and there were strong green night smells of earth and water, and they went to her head, so that she ran along the edge of the lake, all silvery now, to where she knew the Time Gypsies would be waiting.

And so they were, huddled by the bank, voices hushed in the twilight lull, though there was no-one but herself to hear. As she came near she saw that there were two boats waiting, and Granny Porter, Old Mazy and Gil were already seated in one of them.

"She's come!" she heard Sam whisper. "Told you!"

Old Mazy lifted an arm in salute.

"At last — slipping the net of time!"

Polly hesitated. She looked at the boats, the water, the arched tunnel.

"Dad and Mam — what'd they say?" she wondered. The moment was almost too much for her to bear alone. "But *Dad's* been down in the depths of the earth, plenty of times. Dare I?" And then, "What I've dreamed of — yes, I dare!"

And Polly Flint stepped from the bank to the boat

and was already in another time.

"You're brave!" she heard Sam's whisper. "But I knew you would! Here — take *him!*"

A sleepy Babby Porter was passed into her arms. And then Sam pushed off, and they were clear of the bank on the calm evening water, and the only sounds were those of the oars splashing and birds whistling in the woods. And already to Polly it was all timeless, all inevitable and meant to be, and she thought:

"It's where it was all leading, right from the beginning!"

And when the boats turned, in mid lake, for the fateful move into that shadowy tunnel, she felt not a trace of fear. And then they were in the tunnel.

It was the strangest thing. They came through the icy cold and dark of the tunnel and were still on the lake, but now the shores of the lake were lit by little glowing lamps, reflecting in the water, as she had imagined. And people waited on the banks to greet them, as if they were kings and queens.

She saw Old Mazy step first on to that timeless shore and heard his cry, "At last! At last!"

Then she herself was handed from the boat and was standing, at last, on that long imagined turf, and knew, quite certainly, that she was out of time. Slowly she looked about her and took it all in — the curve of the hill, the little lighted dwellings, the church whose bells she had heard ringing with her ear to the turf.

She saw Old Mazy, his face so altered that she hardly knew it, and his hand being wrung by one after another of the villagers of Grimstone, glad to welcome him back to the place where time would never touch him again.

"How's it feel?" Polly heard Sam whisper by her ear.

Polly Flint let out a long breath.

"It's as if I already knew it, in a way," she said wonderingly, herself surprised that this should be so.

"Come along with me." He led her a little way off, to a clump of trees by the water's edge.

"Can you really believe it?" he asked her, "that you're running free in time? Or does it all seem like a dream — as it seems to me when we go above earth after the May Dances."

"Real... unreal... I don't know. Real, I think. But how will it seem tomorrow? Tomorrow I shall be back with Aunt Em and that awful clock."

An owl hooted in the woods beyond.

"You heard that?"

Polly nodded.

"But still you don't know if you're here — or there... So look. This is what we'll do..."

He drew then a knife from his belt, and advanced to a young oak tree that stood nearby, silvery in the fading light.

"You *would've* been my sweetheart, if you'd stopped," he said. "So look!"

And with the knife he carved a heart in the bark, and then their initials...

"S.P.," read Polly. "P.F."

He stood back and regarded his handiwork, satisfied.

"That'll stand for us both now," he told her. Then, "We've not long. Moon rise, nearly."

And at that moment she might perhaps have chosen to stay there for ever, to run for ever with the Time Gypsies in and out of days and in and out of years, but the hands of the children reached out to pull her, willy nilly, to where the maypole stood in the

146

twilit meadow. Beyond it she could see the church whose bells she had heard ringing from above. There was the pole, garlanded and hung with bright ribbons, and the sky was streaked with red beyond.

The pipes and fiddles struck up, Polly was handed her ribbon, and half in a dream she began to dance. And the dance was "The Gypsy's Tent" and the tune "Polly put the Kettle on", and she was caught up into it and drawn by the music and was barely even able to think, "I'm out of time! Here I dance on timeless turf with timeless boys and girls!" before she was spun, and she felt herself spinning, through time, through space — who knows?

She was at the lakeside. She blinked. She shivered. Polly Flint stared over the now near dark water to the island where she had so lately travelled under the shadowy tunnel. She shivered again.

"Alone!" she thought, and was for the first time afraid. Where were they now, her companions of an hour — or a moment — since? Where Gil and Sam and Granny Porter, and the squalling Babby?

"Back home now. Home, where they belong. And even Mazy..."

An owl hooted. The water lapped softly, birds stirred and fluttered in the reeds. The moon made a path over the lake.

"I'm all alone!"

But in that moment she heard a voice calling, "Polly! Polly!" and the voice was, incredibly, that of Alice, and Polly began to run towards it, and cried, "Coming! Coming!"

She saw ahead not one figure, but two, and the second was that of Tom, and he was standing and walking. And Polly Flint ran straight into his arms and knew that she, too, was home.

147

From that day on Polly Flint — or Polly Don't — walked tall in the world, secure in her dreams, and from time to time rhyming as she went. She and Tom and Alice (with Boz, of course) went back to their old home, with its criss-crossing pigeons in the yard, and fields nearby where even angels could come. And Tom went back to work at the pit, though he never again went underground.

And every year, near May Day, they went to visit Aunt Em in her polished kingdom, and every year Polly Flint came into her own again — queen of her kingdom. She went to hear again the bells of Grimstone ringing sweetly through the warm turf, to run her finger yet again over the initials carved in an ancient oak, and most of all, to await the coming of the May Dancers from their timelessness, so that she, too, might spin for a while out of the everyday, and into the secret world of the Time Gypsies.